THE HEART IS TORN

Cornwall, 1782. Beth Farrell, betrothed to Adam Traherne, awaits his return from the Americas — but she fears his ship is lost. And trouble is now looming at home. Her father has drunk and gambled away his fortune, and fallen prey to the unscrupulous Jonah Peake, who desires Beth. Caught in a web of deceit and intrigue, Beth wonders if she will ever find happiness with the man she truly loves.

PHYLLIS MALLETT

THE HEART IS TORN

Complete and Unabridged

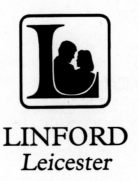

LINFORD
Leicester

First published in Great Britain

First Linford Edition
published 2013

A catalogue record for this book is available
from the British Library.

ISBN 978–1–4448–1757–7

Published by
F. A. Thorpe (Publishing)
Anstey, Leicestershire

Set by Words & Graphics Ltd.
Anstey, Leicestershire
Printed and bound in Great Britain by
T. J. International Ltd., Padstow, Cornwall

This book is printed on acid-free paper

1

Beth Farrell sighed as she dismounted on the cliff top overlooking Polgarron Bay. The sea was surprisingly calm in this last week of September 1782, but the sky to the south-east had an ominous blue-grey tinge to it that warned, to a native of Cornwall accustomed to local weather, a hint of bad things to come.

Trailing the reins of her brown mare, Beth allowed the horse to graze on the lush grass and moved to her favourite spot overlooking the wide expanse of water that gave access to the port of Polgarron. The town nestled in a fold of land that protected it from the worst of the wild elements that frequently raged in autumn in this remote corner of England.

Beth's blue eyes were sad, her usually smooth brow furrowed with a frown as she gazed over the deserted English Channel. She had been coming to this spot daily for more than a month, waiting impatiently for a first sight of Adam Traherne's ship, *Seagull*, which was expected daily to sail over the horizon on the last stretch of its long voyage from the Americas.

Her heart seemed to miss a beat as she pictured Adam's powerful figure. His handsome, weathered features and far-seeing hazel eyes were indelibly imprinted on the screen of her mind, for she loved him with every fibre of her being, and he had declared his undying love for her. They planned to wed on his return and, now that the time was drawing near, her anticipation was overwhelming. She pressed both her hands to her breast, aching with repressed love as she lowered her gaze from the desolate Channel. She surveyed the deserted sand of the cove below, which curved around the water's edge all the way to Polgarron, two miles away.

A lone figure was walking along the rocky shore, and Beth ducked back. It looked like Martin Cresse, and if he spotted her he would undoubtedly intercept her in yet another attempt to wear down her resistance to his amorous wiles. She detested him as much as she loved Adam, and never failed to avoid him where possible, for Cresse was reputed to be one of the leaders of the wrecking gang that operated during the terrible gales.

Turning her back to the sea, Beth gazed towards the grey stone house, only partially visible behind its screen of tall poplars, where she had been born twenty-three years before. She shook her head sadly as she considered how happiness had faded from its portals since her mother's death. Her father, Henry Farrell, was the owner of a prosperous tin mine and three farms in the area, but in the three years since the unhappy event of his wife's death, he had changed from his high state of happiness into a grief-stricken man sinking slowly into despair, gambling and frittering away his fortune and businesses in a decline that could have only one ending.

Beth turned to her mare and took up the reins. Mounting, she rode along the top of the cliff, wondering when Adam would finally return from his voyaging. She was in the habit of going into Polgarron at least twice a week, mingling with the seafarers frequenting the bars and other low establishments along the waterfront, to pick up the rumours that always abounded, and which usually proved to be true when concerning the sailings and arrivals of those ships which used Polgarron as their home port. She had heard several times lately that the Traherne ship would be arriving any day now.

But so far, the rumours of *Seagull* had proved unfounded. Beth put her mare into a canter, painfully aware of her impatience as she allowed the horse to follow the twisting path along the top of the cliffs. The cool breeze coming off the sea stung her cheeks, and the exhilarating ride put a sparkle into her blue eyes, until the mare baulked at the sudden appearance of a powerful figure which arose unexpectedly into view over the rim of the cliff and confronted her with extended arms.

The mare stopped, whirling sideways in fright. Beth lost her balance and pitched from the saddle. Hardly aware of what was happening, she landed heavily on thick grass, which mercifully cushioned her impact. But the breath was buffeted from her body, and she lay motionless while her senses whirled and shock paralysed her limbs.

The figure who had caused the upset came to her side and stood over her. Beth's sight cleared and she looked up into the heavy, pock-marked face of Martin Cresse, who was grinning, his steely eyes gleaming maliciously in his weathered countenance.

'So, Mistress Beth!' he exclaimed. 'I little thought you would fall for me when I decided to accost you. I saw you on the cliff top back along. Still looking for sails on the horizon, eh? Why waste your time on Adam Traherne when I could fulfil your dreams? You know I have great admiration for you, and you would do well to pay heed to me before a bad fate befalls your family.'

Beth struggled to her feet, staggering as she slipped on the coarse grass. She looked around for the mare, which was quietly grazing nearby.

'Martin Cresse, how many times have I to tell you that there could never be anything between us?' Beth spat out with anger. 'If my father was aware of how you besiege me with your unwanted attentions, he would whip you.'

'Your father has other things on his mind these days, good Beth.'

Cresse towered over her, his face creased with barely repressed passion. A powerful man, known for his uncertain temper, he grasped Beth's wrist as she cringed away from him.

'I have a mind to take you as my

wife, but you spurn me as if I were but a weed under your feet. Yet you know you could do worse than me. I would treat you well, and save you from others who would have you.'

'And compel me to live on those poor acres you call a farm, to endure a life of toil and servitude?' Beth was scornful. 'I care not for you or the wicked company you keep, Martin Cresse, and if you accost me one more time I shall tell my father.'

'I would cure you of your arrogance and pride, mistress,' he rapped angrily. 'You know not of the trouble that is approaching you and yours. How will you go on if your family is evicted from Sedge Manor? Your good times are ending, and you will have need of any friend who would be disposed to help you. It might happen that you would then find me attractive, if what I have heard is true.'

Beth gazed at him in disbelief, his harsh words overcoming her innate dislike of him.

'What do you mean?' she demanded. 'What have you heard about Farrell affairs? And who would talk so about my family?'

'Ah, now you have time for me.'

Cresse laughed as he drew her close to his hard, powerful body. His breath fanned her averted cheek and she could smell rum on his breath.

'What have I heard, indeed?'

The pounding of rapidly approaching hoofbeats came to Beth's ears and she glanced around as Cresse released her hurriedly. She staggered as a rider reined in beside her, and her spirits sank even lower when she recognised the heavy figure of the newcomer. Jonah Peake, ship owner and Mayor of Polgarron, was another whose attentions she disliked.

'What are you about, Cresse?'

Peake curbed his fractious stallion with insensitive hands, jerking on the reins and using his heels unmercifully on its flanks. The animal reared, champing on its bit, but was brought quickly under control.

'Mistress Farrell fell from her horse.'

Cresse was hard put to speak civilly, his eyes burning with a sullen expression as he regarded Peake.

'But she is unhurt.'

'It was not help you were providing. More likely you were accosting her.'

Peake lifted his riding crop menacingly and Cresse retreated a step, instinctively raising a hand to protect his face.

'I have warned you to stay away from Sedge Manor and its occupants. If I catch you in like manner again I'll teach you a lesson you'll never forget! Depart now and attend to your own affairs. And heed my warning or I'll flail the flesh from your back.'

Cresse turned away, his sullen gaze boding ill for Beth. Peake turned his horse and rode to snatch up the reins of the mare. His fleshy face was set in angry lines and the devil peered out of his dark gaze. A man who was midway through his forties, Peake, medium-sized and powerful, had thick, beetling brows and a long nose that jutted over fleshy lips. His limbs were sturdy, his shoulders wide and heavy.

'You must tell me if Cresse bothers you again, Elizabeth,' he said, dismounting to assist her. 'That man is not to be trusted.'

Beth suppressed an instinctive shudder as he grasped her waist with inordinately strong hands and lifted her into the saddle as if she weighed no more than a feather. She took up her reins, fighting an impulse to gallop away from him. He remained holding her for overlong moments, gazing up at her with unveiled passion in his animal-like eyes, his whole manner tacitly expressing his desire for her.

'I am on my way to visit your father,' he said. 'Come, I shall escort you back to the manor.'

'I have to go into Polgarron.'

Beth's tone was obdurate and barely civil.

'Then wait until I have concluded my

business at Sedge Manor and I'll accompany you to town.'

He turned to glance at the departing Cresse, who walked to the edge of the cliff and stepped down upon a path to vanish quickly from sight.

'I think I have not finished with Cresse.'

'I cannot afford to wait,' she responded. 'I must get on.'

She set her heels into the flanks of the mare and rode away as Peake stepped back. He called to her but she kept moving, and when she had distanced herself she glanced back over her shoulder to see him mounting his big grey stallion and fighting the spirited animal for supremacy.

Beth was afraid that Peake would forsake his business and accompany her, but he turned the horse away and rode on towards Sedge Manor. She sighed with relief and continued along the cliff top, her thoughts far from happy. Martin Cresse's words were echoing in her mind and she felt apprehensive as she pondered on what might lay behind his utterances.

Breasting a rise, she slowed the mare to look upon Polgarron spread out below her. The many houses of the port were huddled around narrow, cobbled streets, all of which led to the stone harbour nestling against the bay. There was an assortment of craft moored in the sanctuary, but none resembled the Traherne ship, *Seagull*.

Great activity manifested itself along the stone quay. Fishing boats were unloading their catches while gulls wheeled and dived, calling frantically as they sought food. Men were busy mending nets or lobster pots. Some horse-drawn carts were transporting boxes of fish from the wharf.

Beth rode down the long decline and entered the crowded streets. She loved the bustle and apparent confusion of town life. She dismounted at the stable of The Lobster Pot Inn and led the mare inside. Old Jaime Spencer, the ostler, came limping forward out of the gloom of the low building. He grinned a welcome when he recognised her, and grasped the mare's reins with knotty ex-seaman's hands.

'Mistress Farrell,' he said in his usual high-pitched voice, 'I can tell before you ask that there's no word of the *Seagull* this day. Folks in certain quarters are beginning to fear that a mishap must have befallen Adam Traherne. The *Adventurer* put in late yesterday from the Indies, reporting a terrible storm blowing in from the west when she came through Biscay, but no other vessel has showed. There's not even a whisper of *Seagull*. These be fearful days, with autumn taking hold.'

'She'll come home,' Beth said with more confidence than she felt, and a quivering fear swelled in her breast as she fought to discount the alarm that was growing around *Seagull*. 'The Trahernes have all the luck in the world,' she added.

'But luck has been known to run out.'

Spencer spoke with the experience of a man who had sailed the seven seas under the black flag of piracy and survived to live down his dangerous youth.

'Old Jeremy Traherne dropped by yesterday, and I know by the slant of his talk that beneath the surface he's worried about *Seagull*.'

Beth pictured the seamed face of Adam Traherne's father. If tough, old Jeremy was worried then there had to be reason to doubt that all was well with their ship. In his younger days, Jeremy had sailed *Seagull* around the world many times in search of trade, and knew full well the dangers that attended a sailing ship in the late eighteenth century.

'But don't give up on *Seagull* just yet, Mistress Beth,' the ex-pirate consoled. 'If there is one man I would count on against all odds, it's Adam Traherne. Any day now he'll come up the Channel with his holds full.'

Beth smiled and went on along the

cobbled street. She was heartened by Spencer's words, but there was a cold stone in her heart that no amount of persuading could erase, and she wondered how she could continue to endure the uncertainty that had become her lot.

She shrugged away her doubts. Adam Traherne would come home. He was a competent mariner and she had the greatest faith in him.

'Beth, what are you doing here alone?'

A harsh voice broke into her thoughts.

'It would go hard with you if Father learned of your disobedience. I heard him telling you the other day to stay away from the town. You're doing your reputation no good at all, mooching around these back streets like a waif.'

Beth looked up guiltily to find herself confronted by her brother, Nick. He was older than she by three years, but his habitual activities since gaining manhood had aged his appearance tremendously. The death of their mother had changed him from a hard-working, sober youngster into a hard-drinking profligate whose reputation caused the community to regard him with doubt and suspicion.

'Nick, what are you doing here? I thought you would stay in London for at least a month.'

'I got back last night, too late to come home.'

Nick Farrell was unsteady and smelled of rum. His apparel was dishevelled and his blue eyes were bleary.

'I didn't have any luck in the city. It's a bad time of the year, I heard. Father will have to wait until the new year before he can have hope of selling anything at a profit. But you know what those London traders are like. They can steal the shirt off your back without your knowledge, and have the nerve to come back for your coat.'

'Father will be disappointed. He had set great store on raising money from the mine. I was thinking he had begun to rise above his grief, but this news will surely knock him back.'

'He'll never recover. Mother's death dealt him a fatal blow. He's still alive and kicking, but he's dead inside and won't admit to it.'

Bitterness sounded in Nick's voice.

'And you're doing your utmost to travel that road with him,' Beth accused. 'It's time you pulled yourself together, Nick. I could do with some help watching Father but I have to look out for you, too.'

'Don't start that again. I'll manage my own affairs without your help. I was talking to Adam Traherne on the coach last night. He offered me a job, which I refused, even though I think I did wrong to reject him. But I feel the need to sample a change of scenery and I'm thinking of moving to London. It's a fine life in the big city, I can tell you. There's so much to do, and the people there are more friendly.'

Nick turned away and lurched

towards a nearby inn but Beth seized his arm, dragging him to a halt.

'What did you say?' she demanded, her fingers digging into his flesh.

'Say? These days, I don't remember half of what I think, let alone say. Leave me and go home. If you bother me I shall tell Father I saw you here.'

'You said you talked to Adam Traherne last night,' Beth persisted. 'But his ship is overdue. Everyone is thinking that *Seagull* must have foundered.'

'*Seagull* put into Falmouth yesterday afternoon, and lucky to make it, so Adam said. She was badly damaged by bad weather. But the Trahernes have always had good fortune on their side. Adam boarded the London coach and we had a high old time when we arrived here. He's not a bad sort, is Adam, when you get to know him. I never had much to do with him in the past, but we got along fine last night, I can tell you. Now go home, Beth, and leave me to my business.'

Beth stood transfixed by Nick's words as he departed. Adam was home! He was safe! She clasped her hands together and gazed around the waterfront, hoping to get a glimpse of the man she loved. She longed to set eyes on him, to allay the fears that had built up in her mind. But surely he would have gone home to Traherne Court directly to report to old Jeremy. The Trahernes always put business before pleasure.

She turned at once to fetch her horse from the stable, intent on riding to Traherne Court, which stood atop the crest of a hill on the promontory overlooking Polgarron Bay to the south. But a figure emerging from an inn farther along the street attracted her attention and she halted in shock. It was Adam, and he sprang into a coach that was evidently waiting for him. The coachman cracked his whip and the vehicle lurched forward, wheels churning in the ruts of the street. Before Beth could move, it went quickly along the street.

Beth remained motionless, gazing at the fast-moving vehicle. Her impulsive cry of pleasure at the brief sight of Adam stilled in her throat and she hurried along to the stable to fetch her mare, intent upon catching up with the coach and declaring her presence. Business could not compare with the love she felt for Adam, and she needed to speak to him, to reaffirm her love, and to hear from his lips that he still loved her.

2

'Great news!' Jaime Spencer exclaimed, rubbing his hands together when Beth entered the stable. 'I heard that *Seagull* put into Falmouth yesterday for urgent repairs. Adam Traherne was just here. He came from Falmouth by the night coach, and no-one knew he was here until he chose to show himself on the street this morning. He's gone home now, and in a great hurry.'

'He couldn't have been in much of a hurry if he spent the whole night visiting the inns,' Beth observed tartly, her relief at Adam's return tempered by his sense of priority.

Her first priority would have been to visit him.

'He was occupied by business most of the time. He needs to turn *Seagull* around as quickly as possible and get her back to sea.'

Beth fetched her horse and departed, frowning as she paused to gaze along the street in the direction Adam had taken. But the knowledge that he was intent on business affairs weighed against her impulse to follow him. He was planning to put to sea again as soon as possible, and yet they had planned to marry at the end of this trip. She turned reluctantly in the opposite direction and rode homeward, suddenly filled with gnawing doubts.

Riding along the top of the cliffs, she no longer gazed at the distant horizon. Adam was home at last and now she had no need to wonder about him. She left the cliffs eventually and followed a meandering path that led into the trees surrounding Sedge Manor until she reached the main road coming from the town. She passed between black iron gates and cantered with clattering hoofs along a gravelled driveway towards the large sandstone house standing four-square and solid, silhouetted against the bright blue sky. A heavy oak door guarded its entrance.

A horse was tethered at the bottom of the steps leading up to the smooth terrace, and Beth was relieved to observe that it was not Jonah Peake's grey stallion. It was Dr Lampard's black mare, and Beth frowned as she dismounted beside the animal and tethered her own mount. What was the doctor doing here? He never visited socially. Was her father ill?

She hurried up the steps and into the house, filled with an unaccustomed urgency, and halted almost in mid-stride when she saw the doctor talking to her father at the foot of the wide staircase. Both men glanced around, disturbed by her somewhat noisy entrance. The doctor smiled immediately, but Beth was struck by her father's harsh expression, although he was not in the habit of smiling or laughing these days.

'Hello, Doctor,' Beth said and went forward more slowly. 'When I recognised your horse outside I feared something was amiss.'

'You're looking well, Beth,' Lampard replied.

He was a short, portly man dressed in a dark green riding cloak, his weathered face showing pleasure.

'It's merely a social visit, but I have to be leaving now. Widow Belham is not expected to survive the day and I have need to be present for her last moments.'

Henry Farrell held Beth's gaze when she looked at him. He was tall, heavily built, his face bearing evidence of his present grim outlook on life. His height was somewhat diminished by the slumping of his shoulders, which he was now accustomed to doing. His features were sharp, the skin stretched tightly over his cheekbones, and his eyes were lack-lustre, dark-circled and showing strain.

'Wait in the library for me, Beth,' he said. 'I have need to talk to you.'

Beth nodded, frowning. She bade the doctor goodbye and entered the library as her father escorted his visitor to the door. Sensing that something was amiss, she feared that it had to do with Jonah Peake's visit. She desperately wanted to see Adam, but he was putting business before pleasure and she had to accept that, no matter how it hurt. A strange sense of unreality gripped her and she sighed heavily.

The door was closed noisily, and Beth turned away from the window as Henry Farrell walked to his desk.

'What's wrong, Father?' she enquired. 'Jonah Peake always seems to bring trouble when he visits you. And why does he come so often? There was a time when you and he had nothing in common. Now he is always calling here, and his arrogance has grown with each visit.'

'How did you know Peake has been here?'

Henry Farrell gazed unblinkingly at Beth, his hands busy with the decanter on the desk. He poured himself a liberal drink and raised the glass to his lips, his eyes never leaving Beth's intent face.

'I met him on the cliff top. He said he was coming to visit you.'

'Have you been into Polgarron alone, against my wishes?'

'Yes, and I saw Nick there. He returned on the London coach last night.'

'Then why hasn't he returned here? His business in London was urgent. Can he not do anything right? Have I to do everything myself?'

'It is not good news from London.'

Beth's face betrayed nothing of her thoughts.

'What did he tell you?'

'That nothing can be done before the New Year. You have chosen the wrong time to sell.'

Farrell slumped in his seat and lifted a hand wearily to his head.

'Then I am finally ruined,' he said. 'I must do as Peake demands if I am to save anything at all.'

'What do you mean? What kind of a hold has Peake on you? Why is he always coming here? You never had any time for him in the past. He is not the kind of man you would mix with. What has changed you?'

'Times have changed, and your mother's death started the decline. I have been out of my mind since that awful day she died, and my life has been a nightmare ever since.'

'I've seen the changes wrought in you, but Mother died three years ago, Father, and you should be well recovered by now.'

'It was a blow I could not overcome. It caused me to drink too much, and I gambled in the hope that the interest would enable me to cope. But all I've managed to do is squander my fortune, and now there is nothing left, no money and no business. My last hope was to raise money by offering shares in the mine, but it seems that even that avenue is closed to me.'

Beth stared aghast at her father, trying to take in his bitter words.

'Oh, Father, what have you done?'

He smiled wistfully, shaking his head.

'You don't know the half of it,' he

rejoined. 'If only I could spare you the agony that I have made for us.'

'It's Jonah Peake, isn't it? He's at the bottom of it.'

'I owe him more than I can repay, Beth, and I've come to my senses much too late. Peake came this afternoon determined to collect his pound of flesh. I realise now that he was following a vicious plan while pretending to be my friend. He always intended to oust me from Sedge Manor and take over my business interests, and he's finally accomplished that. I'm penniless and in debt up to the hilt, and there's only one way I can escape the consequences of my foolishness.'

'One way? Then you must take it, Father. You can't throw away everything you've ever worked for. What on earth would you do if the estate passed out of your hands? What does Peake want?'

'I can hardly bring myself to tell you. I've been the biggest fool in Christendom, and fear that I have come to my senses too late.'

28

Beth shook her head uncomprehendingly, her mind blank with shock. She had seen her father suffering the loss of her mother, but had no idea what he was doing. His drinking had been bad enough, but turning to gambling, and with a man like Jonah Peake, would be the height of folly. She walked around the desk and placed an arm around his neck, greatly concerned.

'Perhaps it isn't as bad as it seems, Father,' she consoled. 'Tell me about it. I'm sure we shall find a way around your problems.'

'There's no way out,' he said despairingly. 'Peake has won his game of deceit and I've lost everything. We shall have to leave Sedge Manor, and I'll have no business left.'

Beth frowned as Martin Cresse's words returned to her. He had intimated that the Farrells were about to fall into great misfortune. How had he known that? Her mind teemed with conjecture.

'You said there was one way out.

What is it? Why can't you take it?'

'The only decent way out is not forthcoming if Nick's trip to London has failed. I was counting on him to succeed, but it is not to be. I am at the end of my wits, Beth. I've sacrificed all to my grief.'

'You said there is one way out,' she persisted. 'Tell me, Father. We must take any step that offers a solution.'

Henry Farrell leaned his elbows on the desk and buried his face in his hands, groaning. Beth patted his shoulder, horrified by the depth of his distress. He was beside himself with grief and she was powerless to help.

'Peake says he will refrain from pressing for repayment of my debts if I agree to give him your hand in marriage, Beth. That is his only concession. He wants to marry you before Christmas, and if I refuse then we shall be evicted from Sedge Manor and I shall be publicly disgraced.'

Beth sighed long and hard as she considered her father's words, and the last of her hopes died within her. She had always been aware that Peake wanted her and would stop at nothing to satisfy his craven desires, but to strike at a grieving man through his sorrows in order to gain mastery over him was the work of the devil himself.

'I cannot do that, Father,' she said faintly. 'Even though I would willingly suffer anything to help you, there is one thing I cannot do, and that is marry Jonah Peake.'

'I am not asking you to, Beth. I know Peake for what he is, and I would rather lose everything than condemn you to a life of misery with that foul specimen of manhood. Leave me now, for I have much to ponder. I must find a solution to this problem or die in the attempt.'

'You wouldn't contemplate doing anything foolish, would you?' she demanded.

He straightened and looked into her face, smiling wistfully.

'The coward's way out?' He grimaced. 'But it may yet be the only way for me. I have sacrificed a great many things since your mother died, and, in truth, there is nothing left. Perhaps I shall have to consider that final solution. I have no right to bring further distress upon you. I've been foolish and weak these past three years, and I have accomplished nothing by my perversity. Leave me, dear Beth, and I will attempt to come to terms with the stark reality of my situation.'

Beth turned away reluctantly, aware that no amount of pleading would alter the situation. She was numbed with fear as she left the room and went instinctively to the outside door. There was only one man in the whole world she could turn to for help, and she needed to see him urgently. Adam would know how to handle Jonah Peake. A strong man would have no fear of such a deceitful individual.

She mounted her horse and rode away from Sedge Manor, pausing once to turn and gaze at the familiar silhouette of the house where she had been born. Her roots there were buried deep, but she could not bring herself to contemplate marriage to Peake, even if that were the only way to save the estate. Peake was a contemptible man, arrogant and pitiless, and the very thought of consorting with him made her flesh crawl.

She cantered along the road to Polgarron until a lane appeared on the right, and, turning into it, she soon encountered a path that meandered to Traherne Court. Passing through a copse, she was startled when a rider suddenly barred her way, and reined in swiftly, thinking that perhaps Adam had changed his plans and could no longer wait to see her. But distaste filled her when she recognised Jonah Peake.

'I had a feeling you would make for the Trahernes as soon as you learned the reason for my visit to your father this afternoon.'

Peake's rasping voice lashed at Beth, and she detected triumph in his sharp tone. He was obviously certain that his plot was evolving in his favour, and the memory of her grieving father's helplessness whipped up a strand of resistance in Beth's mind.

'Father told me about it,' she replied. 'But if you can threaten him and get away with it then you'll find a much bigger obstacle in me. I would not contemplate marriage to you, Jonah Peake, even if my life were at stake. I would rather die than be tied to you.'

Peake leaned forward and grasped the reins of her mare, his face taut with fury, his eyes ablaze with passion. Beth raised her riding crop and lashed at him, fear and anger lending her strength. A livid mark appeared on his left cheek where the whip caught him, and tiny drops of blood appeared. Peake uttered a curse and released his hold on her reins.

He reached out to grasp her, but Beth wheeled her mare and urged it into flight, eluding his clutching fingers. The mare almost blundered into a tree, and whirled sharply to avoid an impact.

Beth lost her seat and fell heavily. She was dazed, and heard the rapidly fading sound of her horse as it bolted.

Before she could recover, a strong hand grasped her shoulder and pulled her into a sitting position. She opened her eyes to see Peake's angry features thrust close to her own.

'When we are married, I shall take great pleasure in teaching you how to behave in my presence,' he said harshly, his lips pinched and cruel. 'You have been permitted too much freedom, my girl, but all that will change when you come to me.'

'I will never marry you!'

Beth shrugged herself out of his grasp and attempted to scramble to her feet, her senses reeling at the rough treatment she had received.

Peake dug his fingers into the soft flesh of her shoulders and exerted considerable strength. Beth cried out in pain but he did not relax his hold. Drawing her upwards into a standing position, he embraced her with arms that seemed as strong as steel bands, his hot breath fanning her averted cheek. Beth struggled to get free but he held her easily, and, looking up into his intent face, she saw great passion in his dark eyes.

'I shall tame you, Mistress Beth. I have watched you grow up over the years and always intended that you should be mine. Now the time is ripe and nothing will stand in my way. You hold your father's future in your hands, and you will not stand by and watch his public disgrace so you will come to me to avert the scandal that is about to break. Make up your mind to it, and do not make ripples upon the surface of your father's life.'

Beth faced him with anger marring her smooth brow.

'I don't know how you managed to drag my father into your net, but your efforts shall not avail you. I will never agree to marry you.'

Peake smiled, his face set cruelly in triumph.

'You are the one caught in my net,' he said softly, 'and like a fish, you struggle ineffectually. I have you in the palm of my hand now, and can wait for this situation to reach its natural conclusion. Enjoy these last days of your freedom, Beth. When you realise that your choice is between your father's life and marriage to me, you will come to my door willingly to save your father from the ignominy of having to take his own life. Think hard upon that, and you will understand clearly what you have to do.'

Beth was aghast at his words, and shook her head as she turned away from him. Peake made no effort to detain her and she ran, shocked and despairing, along the path in pursuit of her mare. A short time ago there had not been a cloud upon her horizon. Adam had returned home safely and the bright future they had planned seemed ready to encompass them. But storm clouds had gathered, and she was suddenly bereft of hope. Her father was trapped in the sinister coils of Jonah Peake's scheming, and she was starkly aware that she could not ignore the situation and allow her father to sink deeper into the morass of Peake's evil.

The mare was grazing in a dell, and lifted its head when Beth approached. She scrambled into the high saddle and set out once more for Traherne Court, but there was no joy in her heart, only worry and deep concern. Despite her feelings, she sensed that she would have to obey her father to save him, and if the only solution was marriage to Jonah Peake then she would be compelled to resign herself to that awful fact.

But she would not yield without a fight, and hesitated to admit to herself what Adam might do when he learned of the change in their plans. She rode on fearfully, her hopes for the future in ruins, and despair filled her for she could see no solution to an insurmountable problem.

3

Traherne Court stood on a rocky promontory overlooking the harbour of Polgarron. Solid and impregnable, its high walls were proof against any invasive force that might assail it. Beth rode into the courtyard with a clatter of hoofs and slid from her saddle at the foot of the flight of stone steps that gave access to the thick oak door barring the entrance to the Traherne ancestral home.

A stable boy, summoned by the sound of her arrival, came running to grasp the mare's reins, and stood smiling as she dismounted. Beth thanked him and ascended the steps to the terrace, filled now with thrilling anticipation at the thought of seeing Adam. The door of the house opened as she approached, and a tall figure appeared. Her heart seemed to miss a beat when she recognised Adam Traherne, and then her pulses raced.

She ran towards him, and Adam came forward, tall and powerful, moving with the strength and grace of a lion. He met her near the top of the steps and swung her up into his arms, crushing her against his hard body as he smothered her face with passionate kisses.

'My Beth, at last! You don't know how I have longed for this moment.'

He held her at arm's length and gazed hungrily at her flushed face.

'I declare you're more beautiful than I remember. So you heard that I was home at last and could not wait to see me! In truth, I wanted to make Sedge Manor my first port of call, but I have had serious business to attend to, and, as you well know, with the Trahernes it is always business before pleasure.'

'I saw you in Polgarron earlier,' she said as she clung to him. 'You were in a hurry then. Oh, Adam, I have been so worried. Your ship did not arrive on time, and bad rumours were beginning to fly.'

'We had a rough passage from the Azores.'

He carried her along the terrace as if she were a child and set her feet upon the flagstones in front of the big doorway. Over six feet tall, he was a powerful man in his late twenties. His weathered face was smooth, his dark brown eyes filled with an intangible light that seemed to hint at the restless magic of distant oceans and exotic sights that had imprinted themselves in his depthless gaze. His curly dark hair hung over a rugged forehead, and his firm mouth softened as he laughed merrily.

'But I am home now, and we have much to discuss, sweet Beth. Have you missed me?'

Beth thought of the endless months of his absence, the countless hours when she had been the loneliest woman on earth, and her joy knew no bounds. But the knowledge of her father's plight sent her spirits plummeting and she drew back from him with despair showing in every line of her countenance.

'Beth, what ails you? Has my homecoming displeased you?'

He was alert to her moods, and grasped her hands, drawing her towards the door of the house.

'I was about to ride out on business, and planned to call on you later, but your appearance makes me realise that any business will have to wait. We have lost far too much time as it is, and nothing else matters now we are together again.'

'I must talk seriously to you, Adam.'

Beth's tone faltered and she compressed her lips, filled with the cold knowledge that she should follow her father's wishes and agree to marry Jonah Peake. But she could not bring herself to utter the words that would plunge them both into an abyss of misery. She was not responsible for her father's downfall. He had brought that fate upon himself, and ought to rely upon his own resources to escape the net Peake had drawn around him.

Adam's smile vanished as he grasped her shoulders.

'What has upset you?' he demanded, his brow furrowed. 'Have you fallen in love with another while I've been away?'

Beth shook her head slowly, unable to answer. Adam's gaze was incisive, and she feared that he could read her thoughts.

'Are you worried about Nick?' he asked. 'I met him on the coach last night, and offered him a job because he seemed at a loose end. I know what store you set by him. But he said he had irons in the fire. Is he giving you cause for disquiet?'

'It is not Nick,' she said.

'Your father, then? He was missing your mother sorely when I went away. Has he not improved since? Three years is time enough in which to recover from what ails him.'

'Father is at his lowest ebb. I am

43

dreadfully worried about him.'

'Then I shall talk with him and find out how I can help. Don't fret, Beth. I am back now, and we shall go ahead with our plans. Nothing can be permitted to delay them. I have dreamed through the dreary months of my absence, and vowed that when I returned nothing would stand between us.'

Beth allowed him to escort her into the big house, and gazed around with interest for she had not set foot inside it during his absence. Jeremy Traherne was standing in the doorway of a room to their right.

'I was wondering when you would come running, Beth,' he observed with a laugh. 'I've heard how you've been haunting Polgarron for news of the *Seagull*. Well, Adam is home at last, girl, and the waiting is over. You can launch your plans now. I can tell that you're hearing naught but wedding bells now. But how does your father stand on that? When I saw him in Polgarron a week ago he hinted that all was not well with your attitude to marriage with Adam.'

Beth froze at the words, and shook her head quickly as she met Adam's questioning gaze.

'I have no knowledge of what was in my father's mind when he spoke to you, Captain,' she said hastily. 'And I have come now to set wedding matters afoot.'

She closed her mind to her father's problems and continued.

'I told Adam before he sailed that I would marry him on his return, and I have not changed my mind. Nothing has changed, and I hope that Adam is not of a fickle nature, for everyone is expecting us to get wed and I have no wish to cause disappointment.'

'Well said.'

Adam embraced her, and Beth closed her mind to the inner voice that repeated her father's words.

'Come and sit with me and we shall talk over our plans. You can tell me what you have been doing while I was away. In truth, my time dragged so much I began to think that the day of my return would never arrive. We hit such bad weather and more than once I sensed that we had reached the limit of our endurance. But *Seagull* is a stout ship with a heart of oak, and she shook off everything that came her way.'

'Before you two settle down I would like to ask Beth some questions.'

Jeremy's voice was harsh, and she glanced at him to see that his usually smiling face was set in grim lines. Suspicion shone in his narrowed eyes.

'I've heard rumours about Jonah Peake's activities of late, and your father's name was mentioned more than once. To my knowledge, Henry Farrell is not the man to mix with the likes of Peake, so it is fairly obvious that Peake has some kind of hold over your father, Beth. Tell me, is Henry in trouble?'

'Not that I know of,' she replied stoutly. 'His great problem is recovering from the death of my mother, which has occupied him these past three years, and I fear that he is making heavy weather of his efforts. He cannot disentangle himself from the chains grief has thrown around him, and does not seem to have the strength to face up to reality, or even the will to try.'

'Jonah Peake is a villain,' Jeremy rasped. 'There's more to him than meets the eye. I would not turn my back on him in any circumstance. In Polgarron, there is much talk of him these days, and there's never smoke without fire. Peake has got a finger in a great many pies, and I've been alert to his doings these past months.'

'And I need a clear mind for what I have to do,' Adam responded, smiling at Beth. 'Jonah Peake can do what he likes, so long as he doesn't step on my toes. Are you still eager to marry me, Beth? Has anything changed between us?'

'Nothing has changed, and that is the truth.'

Beth threw her arms around his neck

and clung to him.

'This is like a dream come true, Adam, and I want nothing to spoil the pleasure I'm feeling.'

'I have to go into Polgarron to attend to some matters, and you shall come with me.'

Adam bent his head and kissed the tip of her nose.

'I have no wish to be apart from you today, or any day, for that matter. We shall mix Traherne business with pleasure, and see to our business where we can. We have much to talk about, and no time to waste.'

'In truth,' Beth agreed. 'I have a great curiosity about your travels which has nagged me since you sailed away.'

'You will have your fill of my adventures, sweet Beth,' he promised.

'I'll ride over to Sedge Manor and have a chat with Henry Farrell,' Jeremy mused. 'I've been meaning to approach him, but I've held off until your return, Adam.'

'What is happening?' Beth demanded,

filled with fresh doubt. 'Is something wrong?'

'We feel there is, but have no way of knowing until we talk to the men hereabouts.'

Jeremy's voice was low and insistent.

'I have heard rumours, but that is all. At first I ignored the talk, but it seems to be building up to a climax and can no longer be ignored.'

'I shall feel easier when *Seagull* is able to sail into Polgarron,' Adam said. 'Do what you have to, father.'

'You can rely upon me,' the older man replied.

Beth was perturbed by their words. The Trahernes were noted for their courage in facing adversity. She wondered if Jeremy had discovered something of Jonah Peake's nefarious activities, and, if he had, what could he do to end the evil that had been spun around the good, solid people of Polgarron, herself and her father included?

Adam, seeing her doubt, took her

hand in his and looked into her eyes.

'It is nothing for you to worry your pretty head about, sweet maid,' he said. 'Apart from the storms that beset us on our voyage home, I had trouble aboard ship. Two men were hanged for mutiny, and I had word that Jonah Peake's hand was behind it.'

Beth clung to Adam's strong arm as they departed and entered the coach that had drawn up at the bottom of the terrace steps. The coachman cracked his whip and four black horses threw their combined weight into their collars. Beth sank back into the leather upholstery and feasted her eyes upon the man she loved, hardly able to believe that at long last he was by her side. Adam was watching her, his eyes filled with brightness as he took her hand in his.

'You must tell me what ails thee, Beth,' he said firmly. 'If your father has been caught up in Peake's foils then I should know about it. Father says there has been talk, and I cannot help your father if you remain silent. I know by your manner that something is wrong, so take me into your confidence.'

'I should have to talk to my father before I could say anything.'

'Then you do have some knowledge of what Jonah Peake is about. This is not just rumour going the rounds.'

Adam was watching her, his eyes filled with brightness as he took her hand in his.

'Father spoke to me this very afternoon,' she admitted with some reluctance. 'He is in the very throes of trouble.'

'In Peake's clutches, you mean?'

Adam's eyes were narrowed, his face set in grim lines.

'This is the very devil of a situation. I'm home after endless months at sea, and instead of being able to get on with my personal business I must waste time on distractions. But if we are to be happy then we must spare the time to discover what is wrong hereabouts and set those matters to rights.'

Beth could only nod her head, filled with a desire to explain what she knew of her father's downfall, but she could guess at Adam's reaction if she told him. He would probably confront Jonah Peake and deal out summary justice. She sighed. That was not the way the problem should be handled, and she firmed her lips, determined not to speak for fear of starting a series of events which would end in complete disaster for all concerned.

'Jeremy will get his teeth into the situation and shake it loose,' Adam said. 'We can leave everything to him and engage ourselves in what concerns us, Beth. I have been away far too long to let a parasite like Jonah Peake steal my time now I have returned. Come into my arms, sweet girl, and tell me that you love me.'

She smiled and surrendered herself willingly. Long had she awaited this moment, and nothing should be permitted to rob them of the sweet rewards of his return. She thrust herself into his ready arms and yielded to the love that coursed through her body. Her nagging doubts about the fate of *Seagull* were gone, but instead of pure happiness, she was racked with nagging doubt and misgiving.

'In truth, if I did not know what is distracting you I would believe that you no longer love me, Beth,' Adam said as the coach rattled into Polgarron. 'Only half your attention is with me, and I am jealous of the reason for your lack of eagerness. Has Peake troubled you while I've been away?'

She shook her head emphatically, and he gazed into her eyes for interminable moments, as if he would read her teeming thoughts.

'Has anyone else stepped on your toes?' he persisted.

'No.'

She blanked out the incidents of the afternoon, when first Martin Cresse and then Peake himself had accosted her.

'I am sorry, Adam, for my preoccupation, but I am sorely worried about my father. His drinking has worsened these past few months. He has no time or inclination for business, and I fear that everything he has gained is about to come crashing down around his ears.'

'I gathered something of the truth from Nick when I saw him on the coach last night. He explained that all was not well with your father's business. He'd been to London in an attempt to raise money, and failed. Leave me to look into it, dear Beth. If I can help your father at all then it shall be done. I cannot have you looking as if your last hour had come. This should be the happiest day of your life. Your ship has come home, but you're looking as if it went down with all hands. Come now, cheer up. I've brought you a chest full of treasures, and, as soon as *Seagull* gets in from Falmouth, you will see the evidence of the extent of my love for you.'

Beth smiled, reassured by his confident words, but her heart was heavy, and, when they alighted from the coach in the little market square, the first person she saw was Jonah Peake, holding the reins of his restless stallion and talking very seriously with a sullen Martin Cresse. She glanced quickly at Adam's harshly-set face and saw that he had spotted the two men and was eyeing them intently.

'Is there going to be trouble, Adam?' Beth demanded, and he laughed and relaxed, shaking his head.

'None,' he replied gently, then added harshly, 'unless it is thrust upon us. There will have to be an accounting for the attempted mutiny on *Seagull*, and if Peake did arrange it then he will be held to answer for his actions. But I doubt if he can be called to justice. With men like Martin Cresse serving him, he can hold himself clear of responsibility. But we will test his mettle, and if he does not suspect that we doubt him then we might just learn what we need to know.'

'That means there will be trouble,' Beth said worriedly.

'If it does, you will not be affected, Beth. I shall see to it that your family does not suffer. Now put that business out of your mind. You have much to think about our future together. We have waited too long as it is, and I am impatient to set our plans in motion. Put your mind at rest and come along and let me get my business over with. Then we shall be free to follow our own plans. I have much to tell you about my voyage.'

4

Beth was surprised by the change in the weather since her earlier visit to Polgarron. Now the wind was blowing hard from the south-east and heavy grey clouds were piling in across the Channel, warning of the first of the autumn storms that could wreak havoc upon the Cornish coast.

The town looked bleak and unwelcoming as rain splashed across the sloping terraces of huddled roofs and half-concealed the square tower of the church. Adam led Beth into the doorway of a tavern for shelter and they watched the rain driving furiously upon the cobblestones. Beth looked at the forest of masts marking the sanctuary of the port and shivered as she imagined what it must have been like for Adam, ploughing across the watery wastes of the big ocean. But now he was here, safe from the dangers of the sea. She sighed and leaned against him.

Adam looked down into her face, smiling, and his left arm slid around her shoulders. She gasped at the intensity of her feelings, aware that she was small and defenceless in this brutal world while Adam stood square and solid. And yet she was compelled by blood and family to obey her father's wishes, even to marrying Jonah Peake, if that was the only way to save the Farrell family from scandal and disaster. But she knew she would not have the strength of will, or the inclination, to withdraw from Adam. She shivered and tried to quell her thoughts. Adam drew her closer.

'Are you cold, Beth?' he enquired. 'I could leave you here while I attend to my business, and come back for you later when I'm free.'

'I'm all right.'

She leaned into his embrace as Martin Cresse walked by, and trembled when Cresse bestowed a spiteful sideways glance at her in passing.

'I expect to meet someone here from Falmouth for a report on *Seagull*'s condition,' Adam said. 'I did not stay a moment longer in Falmouth than I was forced. Normally I would have attended the ship's business before embarking on personal matters, but I am only human, and I needed to get to you. I have missed you, sweet Beth.'

'These are troubled times, Adam,' she said in a low tone, searching for the words with which to explain what she felt and what might be.

But she could not bring herself to say what was uppermost in her mind, for she would wipe out his happiness at a stroke, and probably set him off on a course that would spell disaster for all of them.

'Trouble, if faced, can be warded off.'

He frowned, gazing speculatively after the big figure of Martin Cresse as the man hurried to get under cover from the rain.

'I have never liked Cresse,' he mused. 'And he gave you some odd looks when we passed him and Peake back there. Is Cresse still working those poor acres he calls a farm?'

'The place stands untended year in and year out. There is talk these days that Cresse works for Peake.'

'Doing what? Peake has an interest in many things, and, I suspect, not all of them honest,' Adam said softly, but his tone was harsh. 'There is only one business in these parts that embraces men of all kinds, and pays a great deal more than honest toil. You know what that is, Beth?'

'Smuggling!' she whispered.

'Never say that word aloud outside your own home,' he cautioned.

His eyes were narrowed and glinting. 'You are aware what happens if folk get too inquisitive or talk too much about other folk's business. Murder has been committed many times in defence of smuggling. It is a way of life along the coast, and seafaring men are only human in these poverty-stricken times.'

'I was only telling you what Cresse is doing these days,' she whispered.

'I suspect he's always been inclined to lawlessness.'

'And now he's always talking with Jonah Peake. But surely Peake isn't involved in smuggling! He's the town mayor, and a magistrate. Shouldn't he be above that sort of thing and set a fine example for others to follow?'

'I'll wager Peake, as a magistrate, has never convicted a known smuggler!' Adam laughed softly. 'He would fear for his own skin if he did, and, in any case, the customs' men would never find anyone to give evidence against a contraband runner.'

'Are the Trahernes involved in smuggling?'

Beth looked searchingly into his face. Adam regarded her for a moment, then smiled and shook his head.

'We were always too busy building up an honest business, Beth, and that's the truth.'

'I believe you. But what can you do if Peake is a smuggler, and did cause the mutiny on your ship? Could you fight him and win?'

'I'll get to the bottom of that business, and if Peake is involved then he'll pay for it. But how to get at him is another matter. I'll wager there isn't a fisherman along this coast that hasn't run a cargo at sometime to eke out his lawful income, or a farmer, smarting from the Government's harsh tax on the export of wool, who hasn't hauled his bales to the Continent in order to feed and clothe his children. The whole countryside is with the smugglers, from the richest to the poorest, all bound together by their code of silence. But if Peake is responsible for my trouble I'll find someone willing to inform against him.'

Beth nodded quickly, chilled by Adam's words as much as by the driving rain that half-froze the air. They had taken shelter in a doorway, but the heavy shower ceased as abruptly as it had started, and Adam drew Beth out of their shelter, holding her close to his side. She was filled with a sense of foreboding as they picked their way through the puddles, aware of the hostility that was never far from the surface of everyday life in Polgarron.

'Thomas,' Adam called, and a tall man, dressed as a seaman, paused in the act of entering an alehouse and glanced over his shoulder at them.

He nodded when he saw Adam, and came towards them briskly, his face set in grim lines.

'Captain, I've got bad news,' he greeted. 'A band of men boarded *Seagull* last night and tried to take her over. We were hard put to beat them, but saw them off in the end, although they killed Tredgett and William.'

Adam's expression hardened at the news, and Beth experienced a cold thrill as she imagined what had occurred. She watched Adam's face, fascinated by the knowledge that he held the power of life and death over his crew and the men opposing them.

'So we were right to take precautions,' he observed.

'Aye, Captain. There are some dogs on the shore who plan to steal your profits. But we have their measure and they won't catch us napping. I'm returning to Falmouth within the hour. Have you fresh orders for the crew?'

Adam looked down into Beth's taut face, shaking his head and sighing.

'It looks as if the fates are against us at the moment, Beth,' he said. 'You'd better return to the coach and go back to Sedge Manor. I have to sort out this business in Falmouth, but I'll come straight back to you the minute I'm able. I'm sorry for this, but there is nothing I can do.'

'Your ship comes first,' Beth said firmly. 'I've waited three years for you, Adam, and a few days longer won't be a great hardship now that I know you're safe. But please, take care.'

He kissed her lightly on the cheek.

'Shall I walk you back to the coach?'

'No. You do what you have to. I'll be waiting at Sedge Manor for you.'

'Tell the coachman to return for me after he's dropped you off, Beth.'

Adam grasped the seaman's arm and strode off along the street with him, their heads close together, and Beth watched until they entered an alehouse, her disappointment complete and a niggling fear rising in her breast.

She began walking back along the street to where they had left the coach, and had barely covered twenty yards of the muddy thoroughfare when Martin Cresse appeared at her side like a black shadow. She started nervously at the sight of him, and he grinned.

'You should be nervous, mistress,' he said heavily. 'Jonah is not pleased with the way you are reacting. If you think the Trahernes can save you you'd better start thinking again. It's time you heeded the warnings I've been giving you. If you want to save your father from what's facing him then you should start doing as you're told. There's much going on in the background that you know nothing about, and although you don't believe me, I'm only trying to save you trouble. I'm about the only friend you have, believe it or not, and soon you'll be needing all the help you can get. Don't make the mistake of relying on the Trahernes. They can't help you.'

Before Beth could reply, Cresse lengthened his stride and departed, and she gazed after his powerful figure, filled with a coldness that had nothing to do with the weather. Her steps faltered as she considered, and she was relieved when she saw the Traherne coach and found the coachman sitting inside. Her relief swelled when she was conveyed out of town, but her happiness at seeing Adam again had vanished completely.

Rain was slanting down again, and Beth gazed worriedly out over the Channel as the coach jolted along the cliff road to Sedge Manor. The sea was rising, the roar of the waves and the wind growing louder.

The branches of the trees surrounding Sedge Manor were whipping and waving furiously in the grip of the tenacious wind howling across the Channel. As she alighted from the coach, Beth instructed the coachman to return to Polgarron and wait for Adam. She felt reluctant to face her father, but entered the house quickly to get out of the storm.

Her brother, Nick, was in the library, seated by a roaring fire, and he looked up at her entrance and watched her silently as she advanced towards him. She met his gaze, and saw nothing but trouble in his expression.

'Where's Father?' she asked.

'He's gone for a ride. The stallion needs exercise. At least, that was Father's excuse. Jeremy Traherne was on the point of leaving when I came home, and there was some bitterness in their conversation. I couldn't catch the drift of what they were discussing because they both shut up the instant they saw me, but Father was angry. I managed a few words with him before he set out, and he had a look of desperation about him.'

'In which direction did he ride?' Beth asked, instantly alarmed. 'You shouldn't have let him ride off alone, Nick. He's in a poor state of mind.'

'I couldn't stop him! And I certainly wasn't going to ride with him in that weather. Only a maniac would willingly go out in such a storm.'

'Where did he go? Do you know?'

'He looked to be riding towards Needle Point, and you should be worried because it's all your fault. You hurt him badly by refusing to marry Peake. You're the only one who can help the family now. You've got to see sense.'

'I don't want to talk about it now,' she responded. 'Can I borrow your horse? I left my mare at Traherne Court when I went with Adam in the coach to Polgarron.'

'Jeremy brought your mare back. It's

in the stable. I'll need my horse. I'm going out again shortly. I saw Jonah Peake in town earlier. He offered me a job and I've decided to take it. I need to get on his right side if we're going to lose the estate to him.'

'You would work for Peake?' Beth was shocked. 'How could you, Nick? Adam offered you a job last night and you turned him down.'

'Don't go on about it, Beth,' he said wearily. 'I've got to look out for myself, for you'll surely do the same. We've got to be sensible about this. Father has ruined us all, and we have to save what we can. The Farrell family is facing a crash, and if we don't protect our own interests then we'll go down with Father.'

'You're deserting the ship like a rat!' she accused. 'Did you tell Father about your plans?'

'I didn't get the chance to,' he responded.

'I'll talk to you again when I've found Father.'

Beth turned and departed hurriedly. She went to the stable, fetched her mare, and rode out on the cliff path towards Needle Point, a local landmark on the eastern edge of Polgarron Bay. The mare was buffeted by the gale, and staggered when the more powerful gusts struck her. Visibility was poor. But Beth ignored the discomfort and went on, afraid for her father.

Presently a riderless horse came galloping towards her from along the cliff, and she recognised her father's black stallion as it passed her. Stabbed with fear, she stood up in the stirrups, peering ahead for sight of her father. She rode on, tense, worried, and eventually sighted a figure sprawling inertly on the short grass of the cliff top. She reined in beside it and dismounted quickly, aware that it was her father, and Henry Farrell was unconscious.

Beth trailed her reins and dropped to her knees beside her father, but was unable to rouse him. He seemed to be deeply unconscious. She sat back on her heels and looked around, the wind howling incessantly in her ears. Then she saw a small figure coming towards her, riding a young horse, and recognised the stable boy.

'Master Nick sent me to keep you company, mistress,' the boy said, sliding out of the saddle and crouching at Beth's side. 'Is the master hurt?'

'You'd better ride back to the stable and tell Tom to bring a cart,' Beth instructed him. 'Can you do that?'

'Yes, I'll be as quick as I can.'

He swarmed into the saddle of his horse and turned it, urging the animal back the way it had come. Beth gazed after him until he disappeared into the shadows. The wind tugged at her, almost overbalancing her with its power. She checked her father again. There didn't seem to be any bones broken, and no signs of injury anywhere on his head, yet he was still unconscious.

It seemed an eternity before she

heard wheels grating, and then a cart appeared. Tom Tredgett, the groom, jumped down from the cart. He bent over his master and then lifted him carefully and laid him gently in the back of the cart, having thoughtfully strewn the floor of the vehicle with straw before setting out.

'We'd best make good time, Mistress Beth,' he said. 'I sent the boy to fetch Doctor Lampard. He should be waiting for us.'

'That was good thinking, Tom. Thank you. I'll ride in the cart.'

She tied her horse behind the cart and sprang into the vehicle to crouch beside her father, pulling the straw around him to keep off the worst of the wind. She chafed his hands, for he seemed frozen, but her efforts were of no avail, and she sat in silent fear as the cart lurched steadily homewards.

Henry Farrell had still not regained his senses by the time they reached Sedge Manor. Nick came to the front door when he heard the cart's arrival, and helped the stableman carry his father into the library.

'Isn't the doctor here yet?' Beth demanded worriedly. 'I'm frightened, Nick. Father should have come to his senses by now.'

'I'm going to Polgarron anyway,' Nick replied. 'I'll tell the doctor to make haste.'

He departed and Beth tried to arouse her father but he lay unmoving and very cold. His breathing was slow and slight, and her alarm grew as time passed. The doctor arrived finally, and shook his head after making an examination.

'There's a big lump on the right side of his head,' he announced. 'He must have struck himself in falling, probably hit a rock. I'm afraid there's nothing we can do but wait. He should regain his senses normally, and, if he does, don't let him go back to sleep again this side of midnight. If he's still unconscious come morning then send for me again.'

Beth saw the doctor out, and when

she returned to the library her father was stirring, blinking rapidly, a hand to his head.

'Father! How are you feeling? Can you remember what happened?'

Henry Farrell frowned as he looked around, then sighed and closed his eyes. Beth shook him by the shoulder.

'The doctor said you mustn't go back to sleep, Father,' she said desperately. 'Stay awake, please!'

But Henry's eyes remained closed, and he began to snore gently. Beth was filled with consternation. Her father's face was ashen, and she feared for his life. But she sensed that worse was to come, for, in the space of a few short hours, her life had turned into a nightmare.

5

Beth spent a long and lonely vigil at her father's bedside, caught helplessly between hope and despair. But as the hours passed slowly, her hopes dwindled and darker emotions rooted themselves in her mind.

Cold, tired, and emotionally exhausted, she sat on a hard chair beside her father's bed until her limbs became cramped and she was compelled to rise and pace the dimly-lit room. Her gaze returned time and again to her father's strangely-composed face.

The grandfather clock in the hall was chiming midnight when she heard an insistent knocking at the front door. Arising, she hurried down the staircase, hoping that Nick had returned. But she paused in the act of unbolting the door and demanded the identity of the caller.

A man replied but Beth could not

make out what he said although she recognised the voice as Adam's. She withdrew the heavy bolts and turned the big key in the lock. Adam came floundering in, buffeted by the raging gale. They had to fight together to close the door, and Beth leaned against it, exhausted, gazing at Adam as he divested himself of his sodden cloak.

Rain streamed down his weathered face. His tricorne was soaked and battered. He smiled though, his expression tender as he regarded her.

'I don't much like being ashore in such a storm. It's much safer afloat. I saw Nick in Polgarron. He told me about your father's mishap. How is he?'

'Sleeping, and he shouldn't be, so the doctor said. I'm so worried.'

He came to her, taking her hands in his.

'Don't worry, sweet maid,' he said huskily. 'I'm not going back to sea just yet. I won't leave until we've married and this trouble has been cleared up. Jonah Peake is behind your trouble, and

I'll see that he doesn't get away with it. I've let it be known in town that I'm going back to Falmouth to be with my ship, but I'm planning to lie low in Polgarron to get evidence of Peake's wrong-doing. I don't want you to worry if you don't see or hear from me for a spell, and I shall contact you when I can. I haven't even told my father what I'm about. He wants me to be with *Seagull*. But my first duty is to you, Beth, and that's why I needed to talk to your father. But we'd better not disturb him if he is resting. Of course, what I'd like to do is spend time with you now, but I must be going. There may be some evil work in progress under the cover of this night and I need to be where it is taking place.'

Beth was desolated by his words. She threw herself into his arms and he held her close. But she sensed a remoteness in him, a mental distance that hinted at his desire to be about his business.

'Can you not stay with me until morning?' she pleaded. 'I feel so alone.

Nick will not be home, and there is only Rose in the house. If my father's condition worsens there will be no-one to go for the doctor.'

'I'm sorry, but I must away. I would give anything to linger, but I need to be in town, and I have to find cover for tomorrow. Don't tell a soul about my plans, Beth. This is a dangerous game to be playing.'

'I won't say a word to anyone,' she replied, stifling a sigh. 'Be careful, Adam. I would die if anything happened to you.'

'Don't worry about me.'

He crushed her to him, his powerful arms entwined around her slender body. She raised her face and he kissed her ardently.

'My sweet Beth,' he whispered. 'Don't look so forlorn. Fates seem to be against us at this time, but the skies will clear, and before long we shall be able to go ahead with our plans. But this trouble has been looming for a long time, and it is better to have it out in the open while I am around.'

Beth clung to him, wanting him to stay. He kissed her tenderly and she clenched her teeth against the pleas that tried to escape her as he turned to the door. A particularly heavy gust of wind blasted against the window panes, and somewhere outside a crash echoed as a tree was blown down.

'Adam, it isn't safe for you to go out there,' she said fiercely.

'We get worse weather than this at sea,' he retorted. 'Keep your chin up, Beth. Why don't you go to bed and sleep the rest of the night away? You'll be quite safe in here.'

'I doubt if I will close my eyes for a single moment,' she replied. 'But go and do what you must. I shall worry about you until we meet again.'

He kissed her once more, and then opened the door. Rain lashed in and they had to handle the door together to get it closed, Beth throwing her weight against it and Adam dragging at it from the outside. Beth locked and bolted it. She peered from a window to catch a last glimpse of Adam, but saw nothing and returned to her father's room.

Beth's vigil continued through the long night, and when dawn finally came she was standing at the window of her father's room, gazing out across the cliffs at the stormy sea.

A knock at the door aroused Beth from her reverie. She sighed heavily, crossed the room to look at her father, who was still asleep, or unconscious, and then tip-toed to answer the door. She was surprised to see the doctor standing behind Rose, the housemaid.

'How is he this morning?' Lampard demanded, bustling into the room.

Beth explained, and stood while the doctor examined Henry Farrell.

'So he awoke just that once, eh?' Lampard asked.

Beth nodded. She was feeling completely drained of emotion, and tiredness lay heavily upon her, making her feel listless and dull. She gazed at the doctor, who was looking at her keenly.

'I take it that you have been awake all night,' he said.

Beth nodded, gaunt by her lack of sleep.

'Then I suggest you take yourself off to bed and get your rest. Your father will be quite all right lying here. If he wakes he'll soon let you know. Rose can look in on him at regular intervals. Eat a good breakfast, Beth, and then go to bed. You'll need to be well rested when Henry recovers.'

'I'll do that,' Beth agreed. 'But are you sure there's nothing you can do for Father?'

'Nothing at all. I must be on my way, my dear. I'll call in again tomorrow morning. Of course, you must let me know immediately if your father's condition changes in any way.'

Beth followed Lampard downstairs and saw him out. The gale seemed to have abated somewhat, but was still raging violently, buffeting the good doctor as he rode away. Returning to the sanctuary of the house, she was keenly aware of the solitude surrounding her.

After eating a meagre breakfast, she instructed Rose in the matter of attending her father, then went wearily to her bed. Certain that she would be unable to sleep, she did so the instant her head touched the pillow, although it seemed but a moment had passed before Rose was shaking her awake.

'Miss Beth, I'm sorry to wake you, but Captain Traherne is here to see you. He's waiting in the library.'

'How is my father?'

Beth slipped out of bed and began to dress.

'What is the time? Have I slept long?'

'It's past eleven, miss. You've been asleep about four hours. I've been watching the master, and there's no change in his condition.'

'Go back to the captain and inform him I'll be down shortly.'

Beth was excited by Adam's return, and hastened with her toilette. She dressed in a dark blue gown, tidied her hair, then hurried downstairs to the library. She paused on the threshold of the room and stared at Jeremy Traherne, who was seated by the tall window. Adam's father rose at her entrance and bowed gracefully.

'I'm sorry to disturb you at this time but I need to talk to your father. I wasn't happy with my conversation yesterday with Henry, and I need to press him further.'

He paused and studied her gaunt features.

'Is something wrong? You look as if you've suffered a bad shock.'

'I thought Adam was here,' Beth responded.

'I'm afraid I have some bad news for you. Adam had to return to Falmouth to safeguard *Seagull*.'

Aware that Adam had not taken his father into his confidence, Beth remained silent on the subject.

'Are you aware that my father suffered a fall from his horse yesterday and now lies unconscious in his bed?' she asked.

'No.'

He sat down quickly and gazed at Beth in shock.

'Do you mean to say that he went riding in that bad weather? Surely that was asking for trouble. Has the doctor seen him?'

'Twice, and Lampard says there is nothing to be done for him. We can only wait for him to recover his senses.'

'And you are alone in the house? Where is your brother?'

'He went into town yesterday and hasn't returned.'

'This is a pretty kettle of fish. Are you aware that there is a plot afoot to ruin the Trahernes? Adam reckons Jonah Peake is behind it.'

'I suspect that Peake instigates much of the trouble around here,' Beth responded.

'Has your father had trouble with Peake? I gained the impression yesterday that he is greatly perturbed over some matter, but he would not take me into his confidence. I beg of you, Beth, if you know anything at all then tell me about it. We are going to put an end to the plotting and scheming that's going on. I haven't forgotten that our brigantine, *Sea Rover*, was wrecked last winter with the loss of all hands, and her cargo taken by the wreckers.'

'I remember it, too.'

Beth sat down opposite Jeremy, and he leaned forward and studied her brooding face, his countenance wearing a ferocious expression.

'Methinks you are more worried than your father, and by more than his condition. You are coming into my family, Beth, so if you have any problems at all then share them with me. I have heard rumours that Henry is in debt to Peake. Is that what is troubling you? I hasten to assure you that anything you tell me will be in the strictest confidence.'

'I cannot say anything while my father lies unconscious,' Beth replied.

'So something is afoot!' Jeremy nodded. 'I knew it!'

Beth sighed.

'And Father may not come back to his senses in the near future,' she mused.

She hesitated, but such was the degree of her worry that she felt inclined to unburden herself by confiding in her future father-in-law.

'Tell me,' Traherne urged. 'If it has to do with Peake I need to know.'

Beth explained the situation that existed at the manor, speaking hesitantly at first, then warming to the task. Jeremy heard her out in silence, his eyes glinting as she laid bare the bones of Jonah Peake's cruel plot.

'So Father is ruined financially, but Peake will forgo the debt if I agree to marry him!' Beth ended.

Traherne cursed and got to his feet, stalking around the room, his countenance dark with anger. Beth watched him, filled with trepidation. But when he returned and gazed down at her, he had reined his equanimity.

'I think we have a chance here,' he said thoughtfully. 'Peake is prepared to take you into his house, and that would give you ample opportunity to spy on him. Once we know his plans we could trap him and bring him to justice.'

Beth was horrified, and shook her head emphatically.

'I couldn't possibly do that,' she said hastily. 'Adam and I are to be married soon. What would he say if I agreed to marry Peake?'

'I am only concerned about the situation that has arisen. I know Jonah Peake well, and I am aware of his capabilities. He runs the smuggling in this area, that I do know, and if Adam sets out to fight Peake then he could come off second best, which would mean his death, or, in the very least, a long term in prison. If you love Adam, Beth, then you'll do what you can to help in this fight against Peake's tyranny.'

Beth shivered, for the captain's stark words filled her mind with frightening images. She was certain that Peake was capable of anything. He had already ruined her father, and Adam would pitch into fighting him without a second thought. But the odds were stacked against Adam, and if she could do anything to reduce those odds against the man she loved then she should have no hesitation in playing her part.

'I'll think about it,' she said hesitantly. 'But if Adam learned of my father's predicament and the situation I am facing, he would fly off the handle without thought, which is what we need to avoid.'

'Adam is away now, and will be for some time. You could get in with Peake without delay, and by the time Adam returns we could have the evidence we need to take care of Peake.'

'You make it sound so straightforward. Others have tried to bring Peake to justice and paid with their lives for being so foolhardy.'

Jeremy shook his head.

'You'd better have a good, long think about it, my girl, and forget your personal opinions. Agree to go to Peake and find out what you can. We'll act as soon as we get firm evidence. Now I must be going. There is much to be done, and I've already started laying my plans. I hope I learn soon that you have gone to Peake. Adam will be proud of you if we manage to succeed.'

Beth followed the old mariner to the front door and stood watching his departure. He mounted his powerful brown horse and rode off quickly in the direction of Polgarron. When he had vanished into the murk of the storm, Beth returned to her father's room. She could not imagine that there was any way she could overcome the menace of Jonah Peake.

Henry Farrell did not stir in his bed throughout the rest of the day, and by early evening Beth was in the lowest depths of despair. Darkness had fallen.

The storm had abated considerably but was still holding sway. Leaving her father's room for a few moments, she was descending the stairs on her way to the kitchen when the front door was opened and Nick entered, followed closely by two men. Beth's spirits were instantly revived at the sight of her brother and she went forward quickly, but her steps lagged when she recognised Martin Cresse behind Nick.

'What is Cresse doing here?' she demanded.

'He's come with a clerk to make an inventory of the contents here,' Nick said. 'Peake has given the word that because Father has not agreed to give your hand in marriage, everything here is to be sold in part settlement of Father's debts. I told you this would happen, Beth. All you had to do was marry Peake and we would have retained everything.'

'Spare me the grizzling,' Cresse said harshly. 'I am about the lawful business of my master and have a warrant to

90

carry out this examination. If you do not give me every assistance I shall report your conduct to Peake and you will be taken to court.'

'I'll attend to this,' Nick said. 'Don't cause any trouble, Beth. We have had too much of that already.'

Beth turned on her heel, fighting down a bitter retort, and went into the kitchen. She sat with Rose, who had prepared a meal for her, and ate mechanically, paying little heed to the food, her thoughts running furiously through her mind as she endeavoured to find a way out of the trouble overtaking them.

She went back to her father's room. Henry was lying still and pale in his bed. Nick came into the room and stood at the foot of the bed, gazing down at his father's immobile features. Beth watched him intently, shocked that he could have gone over to Peake in the family's hour of need.

6

Nick left his father's room, and Beth gazed forlornly at his retreating back, but it was obvious now that her brother was trying to retrieve something for himself from this grievous turn of events, no matter what happened to his family.

She sat gazing at her father's still face, wondering bitterly why such a dire fate should befall them. Her mother's death had affected them all, but Henry had been unable to rise above his grief, and she could not bring herself to blame him for his weakness.

The bedroom door opened noisily and she started up to see Cresse standing in the doorway, smiling mercilessly. The little clerk was at his back, looking expectantly around the big man's menacing figure.

'What do you want?' Beth demanded angrily.

'We have to take account of this room. You chose to ignore the warnings I gave you about what was going to happen to your family, so now you have to face the consequences. You're not feeling so high and mighty now, eh, Beth? Well, you can't say you weren't warned.'

He turned and beckoned to the clerk.

'Make a note of everything, Jim. Peake would flay us alive if we missed a single item.'

Beth stepped forward, barring their way.

'My father is very ill,' she declared. 'You will not come in here. Leave this room. Peake can take his pound of flesh, but Father will not be disturbed.'

Cresse reached out a large hand and pushed Beth aside.

'You had your chance to avoid this,' he rapped. 'And even now it is not too late. Peake would be generous if you agree to marry him.'

'Then go and tell him that I do agree to his terms. Tell him anything to stop this vile business.'

Cresse gazed at her for some moments and the ensuing silence clutched at Beth's throat like a ghostly hand. Her heart was pounding, she felt light-headed, and was aware of what she was saying. But she had to end this situation here and now, and motioned for Cresse to leave.

'Please go to Peake immediately and acquaint him with my decision,' she said firmly. 'I agree to marry him if he stops this awful business.'

Cresse grinned knowingly.

'Don't think you can say this and then change your mind later,' he warned. 'Jonah Peake is not a man to be trifled with.'

'Please do as I say,' Beth entreated.

Cresse motioned to the clerk and they departed. Beth stood at the top of the stairs and watched them descend. Nick was in the hall, and there was a whispered conversation. Then Nick glanced up the stairs, saw Beth's motionless figure, and waved a suddenly friendly hand.

The trio put on their cloaks and departed swiftly. As Beth returned to her father's room she heard the front door slam behind them, and to her distraught mind it sounded like the knell of doom.

She spent another seemingly endless night watching over her father, whose condition remained unchanged. Her heart cried out for Adam's company, and early in the evening she was filled with hope that he might arrive. But by midnight her hopes had died and she faced the bleak night with uneasiness filling her.

At daybreak, she stirred herself to face what she knew would be a day of ordeal. She prepared for Jonah Peake's arrival. Precisely at ten o'clock a coach drew up outside and he announced his presence. Rose admitted him, and he was divesting himself of his cloak when Beth descended the stairs from her father's room.

'Good morrow, Beth.'

Peake was in a cheerful mood, smiling broadly, but his cruel eyes did not display his joviality. They regarded Beth as if he were a cat and she a bird.

'You are not looking too well,' he observed. 'I heard about your father's accident. Is he any better now?'

'Not a whit,' she replied. 'I am still waiting for him to regain his senses. He lies like a man who is already dead.'

'You've had a change of heart since I saw you last. Cresse informed me that you are now prepared to accept my proposal.'

'What would you expect, sending Cresse in here like a grave robber?'

'I think you should stop right there and consider your situation. I am merely obeying the letter of the law in trying to recover your father's debts, and it is only out of consideration for you that I have made this offer of wiping the slate clean if you marry me.'

'What alternative do I have?' she countered. 'I know there is none so I agree to marry you, but I don't have to pretend that I like it.'

'Then let us go into the library and

get down to business.'

Peake was irritated by her attitude.

'I have prepared a paper containing my terms. If you agree to them then your father is freed from his difficulties. I will not press for payment of his debts and the manor will remain in your family until your father's death.'

'You have written that down? Am I worth that much to you?' she asked in surprise.

'I am merely being generous to my future father-in-law,' Peake said and smiled. 'When Henry Farrell eventually dies then the estate will come to me. Your marriage to me is merely buying time for your family. Is that perfectly clear to you? I don't want a reversal of your agreement at a later date.'

'I understand. You inveigled my father into gambling with you and drained his resources to the point where he has nothing left, and you are using his debts to lever me into marriage with you. But have you considered the situation you will bring about by stealing me from Adam Traherne? He is not the man to let you escape with your spoils.'

'Adam Traherne poses no threat to me.'

Peake shook his head, his eyes gleaming, but for a moment he looked pensive, then smiled and shrugged. Beth suppressed a shudder as he reached out swiftly and caught hold of her arm. Drawing her close, he slid his powerful arms around her slender body, and Beth froze in horror, barely able to prevent her revulsion from showing in her stiff face.

'You must try harder to pretend that you like me,' he observed. 'But your feelings do not enter into my consideration. I have you now and you will grow to like me.'

He led the way into the library and seated himself at the desk by the window. Beth stood at his side, her eyes blurred with unshed tears. Peake produced two sheets of paper which stated that he would make no effort to claim Henry Farrell's debts if the intended marriage between himself and Beth took place.

'This is legally binding in law,' he declared, leaning back with a satisfied air. 'Take your time reading it, and then sign at the bottom under the part which is your agreement to our pending marriage. I shall sign it as well, and you will keep one of the copies.'

Beth hardly read the document, her mind subservient to a ferment of conflicting emotions. She wished Adam could arrive at this very moment and rescue her from what was becoming a living nightmare. But Adam was over-whelmed by the misfortune resulting from Peake's scheming and engaged in trying to overcome the evil being perpetrated. She signed both copies of the document and Peake seized them, unable to contain his satisfaction. The quill pen scratched as he added his signature, and then he flung one down on the desk and rolled the other and tucked it into a pocket.

'You have the rest of the morning to pack your immediate possessions,' he said vibrantly, his tone laced with triumph. 'I shall send a woman who is well versed in nursing to attend your father night and day until his recovery. You will come to my house in Polgarron this afternoon at two-thirty.'

'I cannot leave my father while he is in this condition!' Beth said, appalled.

'You have your proof that I intend to marry you, so you must wait until the situation clears.'

'You will do as I say.'

An ominous note sounded in Peake's voice.

'You cannot help your father in any way except by obeying me. I have you in my grasp now, and if you have any sense at all you will realise that you are helpless. Don't give me any trouble, sweet Beth, or it will go hard with your father.'

Beth shook her head slowly, but the hopelessness of her position was stark in her mind. She was following this course of action because there was no other way of protecting her father, unless she could get proof of Peake's lawless activities and deliver it to Jeremy Traherne. Only success would bring an end to this nightmare so she steeled herself to go on.

'Very well,' she said. 'I shall leave here as soon as the nurse arrives.'

'That's better.'

Peake arose from the desk and grasped her upper arms, drawing her into a close embrace. Beth saw his hated face only inches from her own and closed her eyes. She could feel his hot, rum-laden breath on her cheek, and fought against her distaste. He kissed her passionately. She tried to close her mind to what was happening, buoying herself with the knowledge that the sooner she discovered his secrets the sooner she would be rid of him.

Releasing her, Peake turned away. Beth followed him into the hall and was relieved when he fetched his cloak preparatory to leaving.

'I have much to do,' he said, 'and very little time in which to do it. But I shall be at home in the early afternoon and will expect your arrival. Whatever you do, don't disappoint me.'

Beth nodded, and was relieved when he departed. But the slam of the door echoed in her heart, piercing her with a grim reminder of the pitiless situation in which she found herself. She instructed Rose to pack her personal belongings in a trunk, then returned to her father's room.

'Oh, Father!' she exclaimed. 'Thank heaven you have no idea of what I am about to do. I hope this evil will be removed before you recover.'

She sat down beside his bed and rubbed Henry's limp hands, gazing at his ashen face and praying that he would soon regain his senses.

The morning passed and Beth began to suffer the tortures of fear as the hour of her departure neared. When there was a knocking at the front door she tiptoed to the top of the stairs and saw

Rose admitting a middle-aged woman, who set down a large box and began to remove her coat and hat. Nick entered the house at that moment, and Beth experienced a pang of hope that somehow he would be able to help her. As she descended the stairs, Nick smiled at her.

'I've brought Mistress Appleyard, who will take care of Father now you are leaving,' Nick said. 'I'm glad you've come to your senses, Beth. It would have been terrible if Peake had taken possession of the manor.'

'And that's all it means to you,' she responded bitterly. 'I've saved the roof over your head and you give not a second thought to my plight.'

He shrugged.

'It's no use kicking against what has to be. If you're ready, I'll drive you back to Peake's. I brought Mrs Appleyard, and have instructions to take you back with me.'

'Will you stay here and watch over Father?' she implored.

'I can't do that. Father brought this trouble down upon us, and he will have to face the consequences when he awakes. There is no way we can resist Peake so we have to make the best of it, and for you, marrying Peake is a small price to pay to save Sedge Manor.'

Beth went to the door and left the house without looking back. Descending the terrace steps, she entered Jonah Peake's big coach. Nick and the coach driver carried down her trunk and stowed it aboard the coach. Then they departed. Beth sat silent on the trip into town, and when Nick attempted to converse with her, she pointedly ignored him until he finally gave up trying and lapsed into silence.

Rain lashed the coach as it halted at the front door of Peake's mansion, which stood in the main street leading to the harbour overlooking Polgarron Bay. The house was surrounded by trees encompassed by a high wall, and iron gates shut off the driveway from the street. The driver humped Beth's trunk into the house while Nick went ahead with Beth.

The housekeeper confronted them at the door. She was a tall, thin woman with a permanently sour expression on her gaunt face. Dressed in funereal black from head to toe, she sniffed as she gazed at Beth with bird-like brown eyes that were expressionless. Beth returned the gaze with a chill stare, not feeling disposed to be friendly.

'This is Mrs Fetters,' Nick said by way of introduction. 'She has been the housekeeper here for many years.'

'Miss Peake is in the drawing-room.'

Mrs Fetters spoke in an impersonal tone.

'I am to escort you into her presence on your arrival. Follow me.'

The housekeeper crossed the hall to a door opposite, and Nick gave Beth a little push to get her moving in the same direction. Beth bestowed a withering glance upon her brother and followed the housekeeper into a long, well-furnished room that had two tall windows overlooking the bay. Glancing through the nearest window, Beth then looked around the room and saw a middle-aged lady seated in an easy chair beside a roaring fire. Jonah Peake's sister was dressed in a plain dark-blue gown.

'I am Matilda Peake and you are Elizabeth Farrell.'

She motioned with her hand and the housekeeper sat down on a seat by the window.

'Come and sit by the fire,' she continued in a tone which indicated that she would suffer no disobedience. 'Jonah hoped to be here to greet you but had to go out on business, so we will wait together for his return. I must say that I am overwhelmed with shock at this turn of events.'

There was no warmth in Matilda's voice, and her wrinkled face was impassive. Beth was finding it difficult to contain her displeasure. Accustomed to complete freedom of movement, she was irritated by the overcrowding sense of being confined against her will in this big house with its sombre atmosphere. But there was nothing she could do about the situation, and was aware that she had to make the best of it.

'If a room has been readied for me then I should like to see it now,' she said firmly.

Matilda regarded her bleakly, then nodded, and the alert Mrs Fetters rose and walked to the door. Matilda waved a hand in Beth's direction, dismissing her summarily, and turned her head to gaze through the window. Beth suppressed a sigh and followed the housekeeper from the room.

'Your trunk will be brought up when Cresse returns,' Mrs Fetters said as she led the way up the dark oak staircase.

Beth suppressed a shiver at the mention of Cresse's name and a sense of hopelessness enveloped her as she was shown into a spacious room. A fire was burning in a large grate, and the room was tastefully decorated, showing the touch of a feminine hand. A large bed was situated between two tall windows overlooking the bay.

'This will be your room until your marriage.'

Mrs Fetters remained aloof both in speech and manner.

Beth turned to look from the window, showing her back in silent disapproval of the situation, and she remained motionless until the door closed behind the housekeeper. Then she sank down upon the bed and looked around the room as if it were a cell. Her hopes sank.

How could she follow Jeremy Traherne's suggestion of getting evidence of Jonah Peake's wrong-doing? With those two odious women around, she would have no opportunity to pry into Peake's affairs. Mrs Fetters seemed more of a gaoler than a housekeeper, and as the thought struck her, Beth arose and went to the door, expecting to find it locked, but it opened to her touch. She peered out into the long corridor, relieved to find it deserted although she feared that Mrs Fetters would not be far away.

Yet she knew Peake had no need to lock her in. She was bound to him by circumstances much stronger than locks and bolts. She thought of her father, and her spirit began to revive. There was much more at stake here than her personal liberty. Her father's future was dependent upon her determination, and she feared for Adam, who was in mortal danger.

Bolstered by her thoughts, she left the room and walked along the corridor, wanting to familiarise herself with the layout of the big, rambling house. She wondered if she would become the mistress here if her marriage to Peake eventually went ahead, but thinking of Matilda, she feared that the woman would not relinquish her grasp on the household.

She opened door after door, looking fearlessly into rooms to ascertain the roosting places of Peake and his sister. She found the room next to hers had a feminine touch and assumed that it was occupied by Matilda. Almost opposite, overlooking the front of the house and presenting a view of the town itself, was a large room that obviously belonged to Jonah Peake. It was furnished with dark oak furniture, and Beth's eyes glinted when she saw a writing desk in a corner.

'What are you doing in here?'

Mrs Fetters had approached silently and was standing at Beth's elbow, her dark eyes agleam with inner passion.

'You should stay in your room until Master Peake has returned.'

'I need to familiarise myself with my surroundings,' Beth responded. 'If I am to live here then I need to be able to find my way around without having to bother you. I am sure you have many duties, and I have no wish to be treated like a child.'

Mrs Fetters drew a sharp breath and her lips formed into a thin line. She met Beth's determined gaze then turned away to descend the stairs, no doubt to report to Matilda. Beth sighed to rid herself of the tension encroaching upon her mind and continued her inspection of the house, half-expecting Matilda to come chasing after her, rattling chains. But the house remained silent, and Beth descended the stairs to wander through the lower rooms on her tour of inspection.

She was particularly interested in the library, and with her ears strained for the approach of the furtive Mrs Fetters, she looked in the drawers of a cabinet, hoping to find some damning evidence of Peake's nefarious activities. There were business papers in profusion, but nothing to indicate whether or not they related to anything criminal.

She was standing at the window, concealed from the room by a heavy brocade curtain, when the door was opened and she heard Peake's curt tone as he entered.

'I tell you, Cresse, it must be done now. We'll never have a better chance than this.'

'I disagree,' Martin Cresse replied, and Beth cringed at the sound of his voice. 'I've been nosing around the town for news, and learned that Adam Traherne has returned to Falmouth. He was seen boarding the ten o'clock coach, and he is not a man to confront. Snark and his crew have failed once. They won't get a second chance now.'

'Get you gone to Falmouth and tell Snark to seize *Seagull*. If Adam Traherne is aboard then he must be killed. I need his death now more than I crave the cargo in *Seagull*'s holds.'

'All I'm saying is it's too risky,' Cresse protested.

'This is the time for being bold. Go and do it, or get back to your farm. I need forceful men around me at this time.'

Cresse departed, and Beth, still hidden, froze in horror at what she had overheard.

7

Beth heard Peake cross the room and open a drawer. She risked a peep around the heavy curtain and saw him standing at his desk, holding a thin sheaf of papers. Her mind was buzzing with what had passed between Peake and Cresse, and a fierce impatience boiled up inside her. She needed to get to Traherne Court now to warn Jeremy of what she had learned. If proof was what they needed then the orders Peake had given Cresse were more than sufficient. Adam was to be murdered in Falmouth!

A degree of calm returned to her when she recalled that Adam had not gone to Falmouth, but she wondered where he was in Polgarron. He needed the warning, not Jeremy, but she fancied that she would not find him, and someone had to be informed of

Peake's ghastly plot.

She cringed back into cover when the door of the room was opened. Mrs Fetters spoke, using an ingratiating tone that offended Beth's ears.

'Elizabeth Farrell is here, Master Peake,' the housekeeper said. 'She is not in her room at the moment but wandering around the house.'

'What's wrong with that?' Peake demanded. 'She needs to find her way around. I want her settled in here as quickly as possible, and your task is to ensure her happiness. Just remember that she is a guest here, and soon to be my wife. Where is she now? I need to talk to her.'

'She was looking in the bedrooms when I last saw her.'

'Then go and tell her that I wish to see her in here.' He paused, then said, 'No, wait. I'll find her myself.'

Beth peeped around the curtain and saw Peake ushering Mrs Fetters out of the room. He departed with her, closing the door firmly. Waiting several moments, Beth went to the door and opened it a fraction, peering into the hall. She saw Peake disappearing up the staircase and looked around for Mrs Fetters. Thankfully, the woman was nowhere to be seen, and Beth, afraid of being discovered in the library and suspected of eavesdropping, slipped out and closed the door silently.

'What are you doing there?' Mrs Fetters demanded, and Beth turned swiftly to see the housekeeper emerging from the nearby drawing-room.

'I thought I heard Jonah,' Beth said, her heart was pounding. 'Is he in the library?'

'He's gone upstairs to look for you.'

She turned and went back into the drawing-room, her shoulders stiff as she failed to control her hostile manner.

Beth could hear Peake upstairs, calling her name, and she hurried to the front door. If she was to pass on what she had overheard then she needed to get away immediately. The door opened to her touch, which surprised her, and she turned and ran along the driveway to the street. The wind tore at her, but she ignored the elements and went on, wondering if she should search for Adam or make for Traherne Court to warn Jeremy. She staggered into the doorway of a warehouse, pausing to regain her breath. She looked around, wondering how she could hope to outwit a man like Jonah Peake.

She shivered, not being particularly well dressed for the weather, and was about to go on, intending to make for Traherne Court, when the warehouse door at her back creaked open, startling her. She half-turned, and a cry of consternation escaped her when she saw Martin Cresse emerging, a grin of pleasure on his coarse features.

Beth turned to flee but Cresse seized her by an arm and pulled her through the open doorway into the warehouse. Retaining his grasp, he paused and peered around the street, satisfying himself that they had not been seen. Then he laughed, holding her firmly as she struggled ineffectually to get free. He dragged her inside the warehouse and locked the door.

'Providence is smiling upon me,' he said, his eyes gleaming. 'What are you doing here, Beth? I thought you would be tucked up comfortably with Peake at this moment, instead of roaming the streets like a waif.'

'Let me go!' Beth exclaimed and struggled to break his powering grip. 'How dare you lay a hand on me! Jonah will take a whip to you when I tell him of this.'

'Does he know you've left his house? I'll wager he doesn't. Methinks you're having second thoughts about the marriage, and if you're feeling that strongly about it I'll help you get away from him at a price.'

'Certainly not. I've made a pact with Jonah and I'll stand by my word. You talk as if I were a prisoner in the house, but I am free to come and go as I please. Now unhand me, and I'll not report this to Jonah.'

'I'll not take your word for it, knowing what Peake has told me of the situation. He wouldn't let you out of his sight for a moment until after the wedding, so you have run away. That's interesting. My duty is to haul you back to him, but I'm open to bargaining if you've no wish to return. Where were you going when I caught you?'

'Nowhere in particular. I needed air, and Matilda and Mrs Fetters make poor company.'

'I can tell you're lying.'

Cresse thrust his face close to Beth's and she cringed away, pulling against him, but his superior strength told against her, until she suddenly changed her tactics and thrust her slender weight against him.

Cresse went backwards in surprise. His heels found a bale of cloth lying on the floor and he sprawled and fell on his back. His head struck the rough boards with a thud and he rolled against the inside of the door, blocking it. Beth took to her heels, running through the warehouse, dodging around the stacks of merchandise as she looked for another exit.

The interior of the building was dim and she searched desperately for a means of escape, only to discover that there was not another way out. She paused to catch her breath, straining her ears for sound. She heard nothing. She eventually reached the rear of the building and found only a small door in an otherwise blank wall.

Trying the door, which opened easily, Beth peered into an office where dim light entered through a skylight high overhead. She looked around, and saw immediately a ship's bell standing on a corner of a desk. She approached the desk. There was barely enough light but she managed to read the name *Endeavour* etched into the bell.

The name struck a chord in Beth's mind and she frowned as she considered. Then it came to her. *Endeavour* was the name of a ship that had been wrecked two years before with the loss of all hands. But how had the bell found its way here? Had the wreckers taken it before the ship foundered? She touched the cold metal, her mind flitting over the dark suspicions that came to her.

Opening a drawer in the desk, Beth saw a number of ship's log books and lifted them out for examination. The first one belonged to the brig, *Sea Rover*, which she knew was a Traherne ship that had been wrecked the previous winter, again with the loss of all hands. Frozen with cold disbelief, she checked the other log books, and realised that all of them belonged to ships that had been wrecked in the past few years. What were they doing in Jonah Peake's warehouse?

She heard a commotion at her back and realised that Cresse was now searching for her, calling her name and uttering threats of what he would do if she did not reveal herself. Beth left the office and found a narrow opening between two tall heaps of sacks. She wriggled in behind them, pressing against the back wall of the warehouse. Cresse sounded very close, and he was angry. She ducked as he passed by.

'If you don't come out I'll lock you in,' he shouted. 'No-one knows you're here. I'm going to Falmouth shortly, and I won't be back for several days. Come out now or I'll leave you to rot. It's your choice, and you don't have much time.'

Beth held her breath and waited, the silence heavy against her ears. She could feel a cold draught playing on the back of her neck and placed her hand on the wall to find a crack in the woodwork. She glanced around in the gloom, running her fingers over the area and, feeling a slight protuberance, pressed it. A panel slid sideways, permitting a blast of cold air to envelop her. She could hear the sea roaring in the distance, and a dank, marine smell assailed her nostrils as she gazed into the darkness beyond the panel.

Fear stabbed through her and she

hastily pressed the spot that had operated the panel. It slid back into position and Beth moved away quickly, her heart pounding. She could hear Cresse making his way back to the exit and left her hiding place to follow at a distance. When she could see Cresse standing with his back to the heavy door, she crouched and watched him, not believing his threat to leave her locked inside. But his patience was ebbing fast, and within a few moments he departed, slamming the door at his back and locking it.

Beth waited, fearing a trick, aware that Cresse was a cunning man. She moved to the inside of the door and pressed against it, listening, certain that he would be outside waiting for her nerve to fail. She heard nothing but the moaning of the wind. The warehouse creaked and groaned under the ferocious blasts of the gale, a frightening place as twilight crept in.

Presently, she heard heavy footsteps approaching from somewhere inside the building and crouched down against the door, her nerve failing. Suspense built up in her mind until she did not know what to expect. Then a tall figure appeared only yards from her and she uttered a scream of terror which was cut off as rough hands seized her and Cresse laughed maliciously. He shook Beth until her senses swam.

'Did you think I would leave you in here?' he demanded.

'How did you get back in? I looked and couldn't find another door.'

'I have ways and means. You're giving me considerable trouble. I've a mind to take you back to Peake and tell him I found you running away.'

'I was not running away! Why would I do that? I entered his house of my own free will.'

'You looked as if you were running away. Weren't you planning to wed Adam Traherne?'

'That's none of your business. Turn me loose now and I'll say nothing.'

Beth was still intent on getting to

Traherne Court.

'I'll walk you back to Peake's house,' Cresse decided, 'and if you try to make trouble you'll get worse from me.'

'I'll go back there when I'm good and ready,' she retorted. 'I was on my way to the shops when you dragged me in here.'

He gazed at her for some moments, then, showing great reluctance, opened the door and thrust her outside, his anger clearly apparent.

'Get you gone,' he said harshly. 'It's lucky for you that I've no time to spare today. Anyway, you're Peake's business now and it is up to him to keep you in your place.'

Beth stumbled away, unable to believe her good fortune. Daylight was fading from the sky and she lost herself quickly in the gathering shadows. Too much time had been wasted by Cresse and she needed to get to Traherne Court urgently. She almost ran along the street, intent on hiring a horse from Jaime Spencer, the ostler at The

Lobster Pot Inn. But, reaching the stable, she faded into the shadows, for Peake was standing there in the doorway talking to Spencer.

'Watch out for her, Jaime, and if you see her then bring her home to me. I have a feeling she has fled.'

'I'll do that, Master Peake,' Spencer said. 'If she wants to leave town she'll have to borrow a horse from me.'

Peake turned to leave but halted when Cresse emerged from the shadows. Beth shrank back, fearing she had been followed.

'Haven't you gone yet?' Peake demanded angrily. 'What's kept you? I was thinking you were well on your way to Falmouth by now.'

'I've been in the warehouse, making sure everything is all right in this storm,' Cresse replied. 'I can't start for Falmouth until the coach arrives.'

'The coach might be laid up inland, with this storm hammering the coast,' Spencer observed. 'Have you seen anything of Beth Farrell, by the way, Cresse?'

'Not a sign of her.' Cresse grinned as he glanced at Peake. 'I thought she'd be snugly tucked up in your nest by now. Haven't mislaid her, have you, master?'

'Keep your observations to yourself,' Peake rapped. 'Make sure you're on the coach to Falmouth when it leaves, and if it doesn't arrive by six then you'd better take a saddle horse and ride. I want my orders to reach Snark before midnight.'

'It ain't fit to send a dog out in this weather,' Cresse grumbled.

Beth drew back into the shadows as Peake turned on his heel and departed. Spencer and Cresse moved inside the stable, talking seriously, and Beth suppressed a shiver as she looked around the deserted street. Usual town activity was non-existent because of the storm.

She kept to the shadows and went to the side doorway of the stable. Peering inside, she saw Spencer and Cresse in the office. Spencer was drinking from a bottle. She sneaked into the stable and began saddling a horse. When the horse was ready she led it out of the stall and mounted, intending to gallop out through the doorway and lose herself in the shadows before anyone could stop her.

She had started forward when Spencer emerged from the office and saw her moving towards the door. He shouted, and Cresse ran out of the office. Beth spurred the horse but both men blocked the doorway and extended their arms, barring the way. Beth kicked the horse with her heels, but, instead of running, the animal halted in its tracks and Beth was sent sliding out of the saddle. She hit the ground on her feet but lost her balance as the horse shied away. The next instant, Cresse had run forward and grasped her, dragging her to her feet.

'You again!' he declared angrily. 'This time I'm taking you to Peake.'

'Let me go,' Beth pleaded.

'You've made your choice,' Cresse said, 'so you can stick with it. Come on, and don't give me any more trouble.'

He glanced at Spencer, who was leading the horse back to its stall.

'If the coach shows up before I return you better hold it until I get back.'

'If you're on Peake's business then it'll be all right to do that,' Spencer observed.

Cresse led Beth out of the stable and started back along the street towards Peake's house while she grew more and more desperate, aware that Adam was somewhere in the town and she needed to talk to him. They passed an inn, now blazing with yellow light from numerous lamps, and a man emerged from the building, calling her name. Beth recognised Adam's voice, and turned thankfully, shouting his name.

Cresse jerked her arm and kept walking, pulling her along, but the next instant Adam had caught up with them and Cresse swung around, a dagger in his right hand. He made a swift movement with the blade, and Beth gasped in horror. But Adam seized

Cresse's wrist with his left hand and dealt the man a heavy blow with his right fist. Cresse crumpled silently and lay motionless on the street.

'I saw you passing the inn,' Adam said curiously. 'What is happening, Beth? Why are you with Cresse?'

'Please hurry, Adam,' she gasped, 'before someone sees us. Peake's warehouse is just along here, and Cresse has a key to it. We can take him there. I shall explain everything, and there are some things in the warehouse that I need to show you.'

Such was Beth's tone, Adam did not question her further. He bent over Cresse, found a large key in the man's pocket and handed it to her.

'You'd better lead the way,' he suggested as she took the key.

Adam lifted Cresse across his shoulder and they went on. Beth ran to the door of the warehouse, unlocked it, and held it open for Adam to enter. He dumped Cresse inside as Beth followed him in and relocked the door.

'Now perhaps you'll tell me what this is all about,' Adam said in the darkness, his hand reaching out to grasp Beth's arm. 'I was never more surprised in my life when I looked out the inn window and saw you passing with Cresse.'

'Can we have some light in here?' Beth countered. 'You'd better make sure that Cresse can't get free.'

'Just a moment.'

There was a scraping sound and then a tiny flame burst into life. Adam picked up some straw, twisted it into a brand, and lit it. Straightening, he saw a lantern standing on a small table near the door and lit it. Yellow light spilled through the shadows. Beth picked up some cord and advised Adam to bind Cresse, who was groaning and beginning to regain his senses.

'Now tell me what this is all about,' Adam said when Cresse was lying bound hand and foot.

'Bring the lantern and come with me.'

Beth led the way to the office, where

she produced the pile of log books. Adam muttered ferociously under his breath when he saw the *Sea Rover*'s book. Then he examined the ship's bell on the desk, and frowned as he looked into Beth's resolute face.

'How is it that I've been prowling around Polgarron since last night, discovering nothing, and you've come straight to the heart of the matter?' he demanded.

Her gaze was filled with foreboding as she told him about the orders Peake had given Cresse about going to Falmouth.

'And Cresse was to kill you as well,' she said fearfully. 'It seems that Peake heard about you going back to your ship.'

'We'll come to that in a moment. Why were you in Cresse's company?'

Beth explained about Jeremy's visit to her home and how he had thought it would be a good idea for her to pretend to fall in with Peake's wishes to marry her.

'I didn't like the idea at all,' she said worriedly, 'but it seems to have worked.'

'So Peake was blackmailing your father in order to get you.'

Adam's pale eyes glinted as he considered.

'I shall be pleased to confront Peake. He knows that we are betrothed.'

'So what happens now? Is there enough evidence here to thwart Peake?'

'I shall send you to Traherne Court before dealing with Peake.'

Adam sighed and kissed her.

'You must promise to stay out of this, Beth. No more running around.'

She sighed and buried her face in his shoulder, relishing the sense of security that enveloped her. He kissed her tenderly, and she wished they were safe at Traherne Court. Tilting her face, she looked up at him, wanting the tenderness to last, but a distant hammering sounded, coming from the big front door, and Beth's heart lurched in fear as she heard Peake outside yelling angrily for Cresse.

8

'That's Peake trying to get in,' Adam remarked, and Beth wondered how he could sound so casual while her heart was thudding in fear. 'Did you leave the key in the lock?'

'Yes. He cannot unlock the door. But there is not another way out.'

As she spoke she recalled the panel she had discovered and grasped Adam's hand.

'Come. There may be another way. Bring the lantern.'

Adam paused to put the log book of his ship, *Sea Rover*, into his pocket. He picked up the lantern and followed Beth, who led him to the panel. At first, she could not find the piece of wood that operated it, and the sound of insistent knocking at the warehouse door filled her with apprehension. Then her fumbling fingers pressed the right spot and the panel slid aside, revealing an aperture the size of a normal doorway.

'Peake has certainly organised his business, and taken great pains to prevent it from being discovered.'

The knocking at the door had changed to a heavy battering that was accompanied by the sound of wood splintering.

'I think we'd better explore this passage and hope for a way to escape,' he said. 'Follow me closely, Beth.'

Lifting the lantern high, he stepped through the opening into a gently-sloping tunnel that had been cut out of the solid rock of the cliff behind the warehouse. Beth paused to close the panel at her back and then followed Adam closely, fearful despite her confidence in the man she loved.

'Careful here,' he said at length, his voice strangely muted by the close confines of the rock. 'There are steps going down now.'

They descended slowly. The atmosphere was dank, freezing, and the smell of the sea was overpowering. But eventually they emerged into a huge cavern which was partially filled with sea water at its lower end. There was a low cave which, Beth supposed, gave access to the open sea. A small rowing boat was moored there, and the higher part of the cavern was filled with stacks of barrels and crates of all sizes. There were a number of lanterns dotted around the chamber, all alight.

'So this is where Peake stores his ill-gotten gains,' Adam mused. 'And he couldn't have picked a better spot. That half-submerged cave must lead to the open sea. We've laid bare the heart of Peake's business, Beth.'

'How can you sound so cheerful?' she asked wonderingly. 'We have to get out of here, and with the storm outside, I doubt if we can use that cave, even with the rowing boat. What are we going to do, Adam? Peake will be in the warehouse now, so we can't leave by that way, and he'll soon discover that we came this way.'

'We'd use the boat if there wasn't such a gale blowing, but as it is we wouldn't last two minutes. I wish you were anywhere but here. I would have had a chance on my own, but you'll only hold me back. Let me see if there's somewhere you can hide while I take the fight to them.'

'Cresse knows I'm with you. We'll have to do better than that, Adam.'

'They don't know that we came down here. I'll go back up and challenge them. Peake was probably on his own. Follow me but keep your distance, and be ready to run and hide if they get the better of me.'

He reached into his pocket and produced a pistol.

'Take this, and don't hesitate to use it if necessary. Bear in mind that they will kill you if they get the chance.'

Beth shook her head.

'You'd better keep that on you in case you need it,' she said.

He dropped the pistol back into his pocket, took up the lantern and began to ascend the steps. High above them, near the top of the steps, a pistol flashed and the sound of the shot echoed frighteningly. Adam ducked, hunching himself in front of Beth, and she cried out in fear when something struck the rock wall just above her head and whined away into the darkness below. A second shot was fired and again the speeding ball rebounded off the rock wall, narrowly missing them, to screech off another rock.

'Go back,' Adam said sharply. 'Hurry, Beth.'

She turned and stumbled down the steps, head low, her heart beating fast and thumping painfully against her ribs. She stumbled down the remaining steps and Adam followed her, hurried on by yet another shot which mercifully missed them both. Beth noticed for the first time that there was a heavy, wooden door at the end of the tunnel. She caught Adam's gaze and pointed to it. Adam nodded and slammed the door, thrusting home a heavy bolt that was attached to it.

'It will take them some time to break through this door,' he observed. 'But what are we to do in the meantime? There's no other way out, Beth. I must stand and fight here.'

'I think Peake will send for some men before he attempts to get through that door,' she responded. 'Your reputation will make him take caution.'

'Time is the important factor. I wonder if I can get through that cave to the open sea and swim to the shore? There's a sand spit somewhere nearby which is never covered by the tides. If I managed to get there I could scale the cliff and make a run for it to Traherne Court. Then I could return with a dozen tough men and take Peake by surprise.'

'Adam, the sea is too rough,' Beth protested, clutching at him.

'I don't see any other way. Peake won't kill you, but I'm a different matter, so I need to get clear and fetch help. I'm willing to risk my life in the water because I think I can make it. I'm more worried about you, Beth.'

'I'll be safe enough, I'm sure. But you wouldn't last two minutes in that sea. Please don't try it.'

He took her into his arms and held her close, murmuring encouragement and trying to allay her fears. There was a heavy thud against the door at the bottom of the steps and they both turned to face it, fearing the worst. The door was struck again from the other side but was barely shaken by the onslaught. Adam went forward and examined the door carefully.

'I don't think they'll break it down in a hurry,' he judged. 'I must be on my way, Beth. I hate leaving you like this but there's no alternative.'

'You'll drown,' she cried. 'You can't do it. There must be another way.'

'If there was I'd take it. Come and see me off. If Peake gets through that door before I return you'll have to tell him that we parted up in the warehouse. They'll never guess what I am going to do.'

He led her towards the lower end of the cavern, where the water level had risen to completely submerge the cave that led out to sea. Beth could hear the pounding of heavy waves at the seaward end of the cave and saw the rowing boat rocking uneasily in the swell coming through the cave.

Adam stripped off his heavy coat and sat down on a bale of contraband to pull off his sea boots. He looked into Beth's eyes and spoke reassuringly, but she was beyond hearing his words. Her mind seemed to have slipped into a labyrinth of doubt and fear, and she trembled uncontrollably.

'It's time for me to go, Beth,' he said and kissed her tenderly.

Beth clung to him but he prised her clutching fingers off his arm and stepped away.

'I'll see you when I return,' he said.

Before Beth could say more he slipped into the water. She cried out in protest as he began to wade towards the cave but he showed no sign of having heard. When the water reached his shoulders he paused, drew a deep breath, and then dived under the surface. His figure shimmered as he began swimming, and then he dived deeply and was lost to her sight.

She sat down on a bale and watched the surface of the water intently, hoping against hope that he would reappear and clamber out beside her. But timeless moments passed, until she realised that by now he had drowned or was out in the clear and battling those horrific waves.

She rose and began to pace around the stacks of merchandise. She reached the door barring the tunnel and listened to the hammering that was going on with no apparent effect. She fancied she could hear Peake's hated voice urging on his men, and hopelessness filled her as she waited.

She collected Adam's coat and boots and hid them under a bale. Then she went back to the door and jerked the

141

bolt out of its niche just as Cresse lunged at it, a heavy log in his hands. Cresse overbalanced when he met no resistance and he dropped the log and came blundering off the steps to fall in a heap at Beth's feet. She stepped back from him and lifted her gaze to Peake's haggard face as he came striding towards her. Peake had a large pistol in his right hand and he thrust the weapon in her face.

'What have you done?' he snarled. 'Where is Traherne?'

'Adam? He is not with me,' she responded in such a matter-of-fact tone that Peake was silenced by surprise. 'But I am quite sure he is safe by now.'

'They both came down here,' Cresse said. 'I heard them talking. You've got to end it for Traherne now, Peake, before he puts a rope around our necks. And if you have any sense at all you'll drown this female.'

'Keep your mouth shut,' Peake snapped. 'I don't want your opinion on anything. Because of you, everything has gone wrong today. I never had much faith in you, Cresse, but this time you've excelled yourself. Search every nook and cranny, and kill Traherne the instant you set eyes on him.'

'What about her?' Cresse demanded.

'I'll deal with her. Come along, Beth. I'm taking you back to my house, and this time you'll stay there, for if you don't then something very bad will happen to your father. I have taken the precaution of sending two men to stay at the manor, and if you disobey me again they'll get word that your father is to be killed. So do as you're told or the worst will happen.'

Peake grasped Beth's arm and bundled her into the tunnel, forcing her to ascend the steps. She did not resist. Her mind was overburdened with fear for Adam. She could only assume that the man she loved was dead. No-one could have survived the perils of that stormy sea. He was gone and she had the grim prospect of facing the future without him.

Peake was silent as they walked back along the dark street to his house. Beth was not aware of her surroundings, and when they entered the house she stood submissively at Peake's side while he remonstrated with Matilda and Mrs Fetters for their failure to supervise Beth's movements.

'As for you,' he continued, grasping Beth's arm, 'I shall lock you in your room until I have the time to deal with you. Come along.'

They ascended the stairs and Beth entered her room. Peake stood in the doorway gazing at her as she crossed to the bed and sank down upon it.

'Just remember that your father's life is at stake now,' he warned.

Beth did not reply. She sat with eyes downcast, her manner submissive. Peake departed, locking the door. But when silence ensued, Beth arose and became animated. She had to get to Traherne Court and raise the alarm.

Her trunk was at the foot of the bed and she opened it. Unpacking the contents hurriedly and throwing them on the bed, she searched for suitable clothing. She changed her footwear and put on outdoor shoes. Then she crossed to the door and tried it, finding it well and truly locked. But her determination was such that she went to the fireplace without a second thought and picked up the poker lying there.

She thought that Peake would have returned immediately to his warehouse, and hammered on the door with the poker until Mrs Fetters called to her from outside the room.

'I'm feeling ill with hunger,' Beth replied in answer to the housekeeper's enquiry. 'Please bring me some food. Jonah didn't tell you to starve me.'

'He locked the door and took the key with him,' Mrs Fetters replied.

'You must have a key to every door in the house, as housekeeper.'

'I do, but I cannot go against the master's orders.'

'I'm sure he didn't tell you to starve me. I need food.'

'I'll talk to Matilda, so stop banging on the door.'

Mrs Fetters hurried away, leaving Beth motionless. Her determination was at its highest pitch. She dared not think of Adam. Her instincts warned that he must be dead but she dared not think about the possibility. Many minutes later, Mrs Fetters returned.

'You must sit on the bed and remain quite still while Matilda and I bring in a tray,' the housekeeper said from outside the door.

'I'll do as you say,' Beth replied, and went to sit on the foot of the bed, concealing the poker at her back.

A key grated in the lock and then the door was opened a fraction. Mrs Fetters peered into the room cautiously, saw Beth sitting dejectedly on the bed, apparently resigned to the situation, and pushed the door wide. Matilda entered the room carrying a tray and Mrs Fetters advanced with her.

Beth arose and produced the poker. She brandished it and darted to the

door while both women stood transfixed in shock. In a trice she was out of
the room, and paused only to slam the
door and turn the key protruding from
the lock. She descended the stairs and
crossed the hall. Unlocking the front
door, she left it open and fled into the
night.

Reaching the deserted, rain-swept
street, Beth paused to consider. She
needed to pass on her information to
Jeremy Traherne but found herself
reluctant to leave the town in case
Adam had succeeded in escaping from
the cave and had swum ashore. If he
had managed it then he would even
now be raising an alarm and men
would be gathering nearby to assail
Peake. But the town was deathly still
and quiet.

Beth hurried along the street towards
Peake's warehouse, staying in the shadows. She was still gripping the poker in
her hand. Reaching the building, she
was disappointed to find it silent and in
complete darkness. She pushed against

the door to find that it was locked. She peered into the surrounding shadows.

She realised that there was nothing for it but to make for Traherne Court, and she did not relish the long walk. But she did not know who in Polgarron she could trust, and set out back along the street, determined to do what was necessary to bring Peake to justice.

She reached the inn that Adam had emerged from when she had passed earlier with Cresse, and paused to peer into the bright interior. If only Adam were here now! She shook her head sadly as the thought flitted through her mind. Stiffening her resolve, she prepared to go on, but the door of the inn was opened at that moment and a man and a woman emerged. Beth shrank into the shadows while they paused, talking, and then they went on along the street ahead of her.

Beth let them draw clear before moving in the same direction. She intended leaving town as quickly as possible. When the pair paused at the door of a house she waited for them to enter. The woman opened the door and lamplight streamed out, bathing the man. Beth froze — it was Adam.

She tried to call out but her tongue seemed glued in her mouth. He looked around fearfully as the light enveloped him, then moved hurriedly into the shadows. The next instant he was gone, and the woman went into the house and closed the door. Beth drew a deep breath, wondering if she had imagined the sighting of Adam. She ran forward to the door of the house and peered into the shadows, looking for the man, but he had disappeared as completely as if he had never been there.

Beth stood undecided while her shock receded, fearing for the soundness of her mind, afraid that she was beginning to see Adam in every man she looked at. But she could not have been mistaken, and knocked on the door the woman had used. When the door opened, Beth found herself looking at a middle-aged woman, and was suddenly at a loss for words. But the woman thrust her face forward and peered intently at Beth.

'I know you,' she declared. 'You're Elizabeth Farrell. What are you doing out on such a night?'

'I saw you coming home,' Beth said. 'Who was the man with you?'

'Man? I wasn't with no man, dearie. My husband is at sea. I wouldn't dare look at another man for fear that Rufus would find out.'

'The man you came out of the inn with,' Beth insisted. 'He left you at this door. It was Adam Traherne, wasn't it? I must know. Please tell me.'

As she spoke, Beth felt a weakness begin to overwhelm her, and a strange roaring sound filled her ears. She staggered, and would have fallen if the woman had not reached out to grasp her.

'Here, you'd better come inside and sit down for a moment,' the woman said worriedly. 'You're all in. What have you been doing with yourself?'

Beth allowed herself to be helped into the house. She closed her eyes against sickening dizziness, and the woman's voice became fainter then faded into silence as Beth collapsed into the woman's arms.

9

Beth came to her senses when rum seared her throat, almost choking her. She heard a woman's voice and opened her eyes to find herself lying on the hard floor of the house. The woman straightened, a glass in her hand and a look of genuine sympathy on her gaunt face.

'You gave me a nasty turn, fainting like that,' she declared. 'I thought you'd died on me, as sure as my name is Jane Mull. Can you get up?'

Beth regained her feet with Jane's help and was led into a room and seated on a chair. Jane went to close the door, then returned, and Beth confronted her, grasping her arms.

'You must help me, Jane,' she said fervently. 'That man you were with. It was Adam Traherne, wasn't it?'

'I came home alone,' Jane replied

doggedly. 'I work at the inn while my Rufus is away, and I never walk home with any man.'

'You say you know me by sight. You know I'm Elizabeth Farrell, and I live at Sedge Manor. If you do know about me then you must be aware that I am betrothed to Adam Traherne. He has just returned from the Americas and we are to be married very soon.'

'I know who you are and I saw you earlier, arm in arm with Martin Cresse, who is Jonah Peake's man. My Rufus is mate aboard the *Seagull*. Trouble's building up in Falmouth, and they do say Peake is behind it.'

'I know about it,' Beth said. 'Adam told me. Peake's men tried to steal *Seagull* two nights ago and two of the *Seagull*'s crew were killed.'

'You could have learned that from Peake.'

'You must have given Adam some of your husband's clothes to wear,' Beth continued. 'Adam and I were trapped in a cavern below Peake's warehouse.

There was no way out so Adam stripped off and swam through a cave and into the sea. He plans to get some of his men together and raid Peake's warehouse. You must tell me if it was Adam with you. If he has gone to Traherne Court for help then I don't have to go there, but if it wasn't Adam then I have to warn his father, Captain Traherne. You can trust me. If Peake gets the better of the Trahernes then your husband will surely suffer along with the rest of them.'

'It was Adam,' Jane said reluctantly. 'He came to the inn for help, half-dressed and half-drowned. He'd been in the sea all right. I gave him some clothes belonging to Rufus and he's gone to fetch the excisemen to Peake's warehouse. He told me not to tell anyone that I'd seen him. Will you stay here until Adam gets back? He's promised to let me know what happens.'

'I'd better go to Traherne Court and tell Jeremy Traherne.'

Beth prepared to leave, and felt quite elated as she went out into the storm and hurried along the street. But the prospect of the long walk to Traherne Court did not appeal to her, although nothing could dismay her now and she strode along with great resolution.

She crossed to the opposite side of the street when she reached Peake's warehouse, and was pressing through the shadows when a coach came along and stopped outside the building. Pausing, Beth watched three men alight from the coach. They looked around furtively, then dragged a man out of the coach and half-carried him into the warehouse.

Beth was instantly alerted. She had not been able to gather any details of the fourth man, but her immediate fear was that it was Adam. But surely he had not fallen foul of yet more of Peake's men. She crossed the street and hurried to the warehouse door, found it ajar, and peered into the building.

There was a lantern burning just

inside the door, and by its dim light she saw the three men carrying the fourth man towards the office. She almost gasped aloud when she saw that the fourth man was indeed Adam. He seemed to be unconscious, and she turned away quickly, aware that her only chance of help was by reaching Traherne Court.

Hurrying along the street, Beth turned off to avoid the port and crossed into the dark road that led to the outskirts of the town. She was breathless and tired, but the desperate thought of Adam being held by Peake's men was sufficient to force her beyond her physical limit and she hastened on.

Reaching the cliff top on the southern side of Polgarron Bay, she hurried out into the open. Glancing out at the bay, she could see the torment of the sea. There was a ship riding at anchor in the comparative shelter of the bay, and at times it was almost completely submerged by the rolling waves thundering towards the shore.

An hour passed before she reached the grounds of Traherne Court. Lights were showing in several windows, and Beth had never seen a more welcome sight. She hurried along the drive despite her fatigue and struggled up the steps to the terrace. She fell against the front door of the house, hammered on the thick panels, then leaned against it while awaiting some answer. The door was opened by Jeremy himself, and he exclaimed loudly when he saw her. On the point of fainting with exhaustion, Beth fell into Jeremy's arms. He lifted her over the doorstep and sat her down on a padded seat in the hall.

She blurted out a hesitant account of what had happened, and Jeremy cut her short after learning the salient points.

'Stay here and rest while I gather the estate workers,' he said. 'We'll go into town and enter Peake's warehouse. I just hope we'll not be too late.'

Beth struggled to her feet and moved to the door but Jeremy grasped her arm, forcing her to sit down again.

'You're all in,' he observed. 'I want you to stay here out of harm's way. Go to the kitchen and make yourself a hot drink and eat some food.'

'It will take you time to gather your men,' she replied. 'In the meantime, anything could happen to Adam. I've got to go back to town. I might be able to do something to help.'

Jeremy had no time to argue, and, while he was getting dressed, Beth dragged open the front door and departed, hastening back the way she had come. After an interminable period, she reached Polgarron and hurried through the deserted streets, concerned only with Adam's plight.

A horse and cart was waiting outside the warehouse when Beth reached it, and, miraculously, the door of the building stood ajar. As she crept closer to the door it was jerked wide open from inside and two men appeared, carrying a large crate between them. Beth faded into the shadows and crouched like a hunted animal, her heart pounding.

The men put the crate on the cart and hurried back into the warehouse.

'One more bale and we can be on our way,' one of them said.

Beth eased forward, her pulses racing. She could hear the men talking, and peered around the door to see them dragging a large bale off the top of a nearby stack. There were two lanterns burning inside the warehouse, one close to the door and another over by the office. She sneaked into the warehouse and ducked into cover, quite breathless with anticipation.

The men departed with the bale, and a few moments later one of them reappeared and doused the lamp by the door. He departed again, and Beth heard the door close with a bang and then a key grating in the lock. The cart rumbled away and an uneasy silence settled. Beth gazed around fearfully. She had last seen Adam being carried into the office, and moved carefully across to the inner door and opened it, her teeth clenched, her nerves taut. But the office was deserted, and she looked around in disbelief.

Where was Adam? She would have to check the cavern. Taking up the nearby lantern, she went to the door that gave access to the cavern.

The panel opened easily and she summoned up the last vestiges of nerve and strength. Descending the steps, she reached the cavern without incident and immediately saw Adam lying on a low stack of bales. Bound tightly, he was looking in her direction, his gaze attracted by the light of the lantern she was carrying. Beth uttered a cry of relief and hurried to his side.

There was a smear of blood on Adam's right temple. His face was pale and he seemed to be on the point of collapse. Beth untied him with difficulty for he had been bound with a length of tarred rope. She chattered nervously, telling him everything that had happened to her since he dived into the pool. When his hands were free, Adam sat up and grasped Beth in his arms. She clung to him, her relief overwhelming, and tears coursed down her cheeks as a nervous reaction seized her.

'Beth, once again you've saved me. I was saying my prayers, for Cresse has threatened to kill me on his return. I had given up because I've pushed myself to the limit of my strength. But seeing you has given me fresh power. How is it that you have walked down here without hindrance?'

As Beth explained, Adam arose and looked around. He picked up a short length of wood, his eyes filled with a determined glitter.

'This will have to do,' he mused. 'But if only I had a pistol, I'd give Cresse his ticket to oblivion when he returns.'

'Wait.'

Beth took the lantern and led him to the spot where she had hidden his coat and boots. He smiled as he took his pistol from the pocket of the coat.

'I thought my last moments had come several times since I left you in

161

here, Beth,' he observed.

'I thought you had drowned. I still can't believe you got out through the cave and made it to the shore.'

'That was the worst experience I ever had. Now I'm ready to fight. But I must get you out of here, Beth. Let's go up to the warehouse.'

Beth had no intention of leaving his side, although she said nothing. Adam took the lantern and they ascended the steps. The warehouse was silent and still when they reached it.

'Beth, I want to wait here for Cresse. You'll have to stay in the office until I've dealt with him. I heard him say he was coming back.'

'No, Adam. I'm not letting you out of my sight now. Give me that piece of wood and I'll stand by you.'

Admiration showed in Adam's eyes but he shook his head. He set the lantern on a crate near the door and checked his pistol.

'All we can do now is wait,' he said firmly.

Beth pushed herself into his arms, closed her eyes, and rested her weight against him. She was utterly exhausted, and Adam kissed her.

'We may be in for a long wait,' he observed. 'It will take my father another hour to get here. Why don't you lie down on one of those bales and try to sleep? And you'll be out of the way if Cresse shows up.'

'I couldn't sleep,' she protested. 'Just hold me, Adam. I need to be comforted now. During all the weeks I've waited for your return, I never imagined we would have to go through such an ordeal as this, and I hope never to see Jonah Peake again.'

'Peake is finished,' Adam said confidently. 'We have the proof of his guilt all around us.'

He leaned against a stack of contraband and embraced Beth.

Time passed unmeasured, and Beth was lulled into a half-sleep, protected by Adam's arms. Silence encompassed them like a shroud, until the door rattled, and then voices were heard.

'Someone's left a light inside,' Peake said. 'Open the door, Cresse. It's a wonder the place hasn't burned down.'

Adam put Beth from him and drew his pistol. He motioned for Beth to conceal herself, and she moved swiftly behind a nearby stack and crouched in a position that gave her a view of the door. Adam moved to his right and covered the door from an angle.

The door opened slowly and Cresse entered, holding a pistol. Beth, her eyes wide and her heart racing, saw Jonah Peake, also armed, at Cresse's shoulder. Both men crossed the threshold and paused to look around.

'That's perfect,' Adam said as he stepped forward. 'Drop your pistols and raise your hands.'

Cresse started in shock and instinctively swung his pistol to cover Adam, and Peake sprang behind Cresse. Adam fired instantly. Cresse uttered a cry, dropped his pistol and fell to the ground, writhing in agony, but Peake turned and fled out into the night. Adam ran forward, pocketing his empty pistol, and snatched up the weapon Cresse had dropped.

'Peake's got away!'

Beth emerged from her cover, trembling.

'Is Cresse dead?'

Adam bent over the man, who lay motionless.

'No, he's still breathing. I didn't aim to kill. I want him alive so he can talk. He knows all about Peake's business.'

'Peake will fetch some of his men,' Beth warned.

'I'll stay here and wait for my father to arrive. You must go and alert Peter Radcliffe, the exciseman. I'm not risking your life again. Come on. We'd better leave here and watch the place from outside. Hurry, Beth, before Peake returns.'

He led her to the door, and as they stepped out into the street a pistol shot cracked. The ball thudded into the door close to Adam's head and he fired

Cresse's pistol at the muzzle flash across the street. As the echoes of the shots faded, they both heard the sound of receding footsteps.

'That was Peake's parting shot,' Adam observed grimly. 'I wish I could get my hands on him.'

'It was not my shot,' Peake said from the shadows, and stepped forward, a pistol in his hand. 'I knew your brother would come in useful, Beth. He's drawn your fire, Traherne, and now I've got you. Back inside the warehouse, both of you. You've made a bad mistake, Beth. Your father will die now to pay for your meddling, and his blood will be on your hands.'

Adam watched Peake intently, but the man stayed out of arm's length as he forced them to go back into the warehouse, menaced by his pistol.

'Lie down on your face, Traherne,' Peake ordered, and Adam could not but obey. 'Bind his hands and feet, Beth. You can be useful at last. Between the two of you, you've just about ruined my business, but I can save the situation by taking drastic action. I shall destroy the evidence here, and you two with it.'

Beth paused in knotting the rope she was binding around Adam's wrists, and Peake laughed mirthlessly as he met her frightened gaze.

'Finish tying him,' he rasped. 'I'm not a fool, Beth. I had no idea you were so in love with Traherne, but you've proved it this night. So I must cut my losses. I shall have to forgo the pleasure of your company during the remainder of my days. You know too much to be trusted.'

He moved to Beth's side and bent to test the knots she had tied in the rope binding Adam. Satisfied, he pushed her aside and bound Adam's legs securely.

'Now it is your turn, Beth. Lie down.'

Peake thrust her on to the bales beside Adam and bound her hand and foot. Then he stepped back, smiling.

'It's such a waste,' he mused, 'but there is no help for it.'

Beth watched Peake as he crossed to

the office. He collected the lantern there, and a devilish expression occupied his face as he fetched two other lanterns and lit them.

'You may wonder what I am about, Beth,' Peake said. 'There's only one way I can remove the evidence of my guilt in the short time I have left, and that is by fire. The storm will ensure a healthy blaze.'

'Help me out of here, Peake,' Cresse's voice could be heard suddenly.

Beth looked at Cresse, lying close by, and saw that he had propped himself up on one elbow, his face ghastly pale in the lantern light. Blood was soaking his coat. He held out a hand pleadingly.

'You're finished, too, Cresse,' Peake snarled. 'You've been such a bungler I shall be well rid of you. You can die with these two!'

As he lapsed into silence, Peake took one of the lanterns, walked to a nearby stack of bales, and threw the lantern against the base of the stack. The glass smashed and oil splashed over the bales, igniting instantly and spreading fire quickly. Peake did the same with the other two lanterns, and fire began to spread, crackling furiously.

Peake paused as smoke began to fill the warehouse. He gazed down at Beth, who looked imploringly at him, then turned on his heel and departed, slamming the big door. Beth heard the key grating in the lock.

'Adam,' she gasped. 'What can we do?'

'Cresse,' Adam called, 'can you move? If you can, crawl over here and untie me. It's our only chance. Those flames are spreading fast.'

Beth looked at Cresse, who was already inching towards them along the ground. He was groaning at each movement, his ashen face twisted in pain. Thankfully, he was very close to where they lay bound, and within a few moments he was leaning over Beth. He drew a knife from the sheath on his belt and paused to gaze at her, breathing shallowly and in much pain.

'You wouldn't heed my warnings,' he said weakly. 'I could have saved you much of this, Beth. Traherne, Peake has deserted me so I'll set you free if you promise that he'll pay for this.'

'He'll pay,' Adam rapped. 'You can count on that. Hurry, Cresse. The fire is taking hold.'

Once free, Adam ran to the door, tried it without success and turned to seize one of several barrels stacked nearby. He rained a series of blows against the big lock while Beth stood at his shoulder, gasping and coughing. In a few moments the lock yielded and the door swung open.

'Outside, quickly, Beth.'

Adam turned and ran into the smoke to get Cresse as Beth staggered outside into the fresh air.

10

Adam came staggering out of the warehouse with Cresse across his shoulders. He cleared the building and laid his burden on the ground.

'Cresse is dead, Beth,' he said softly.

Beth was shocked.

'He saved our lives,' she said shakily.

Adam turned and looked at the warehouse. Smoke was billowing out through the front door and there was the ominous red glow of a fire out of control. A man ran along the street to halt beside them.

'You'd better raise the alarm,' Adam said to him. 'In this gale, that fire could burn down the whole town.'

The man stared at Adam, then, without a word, turned and ran back along the street, yelling at the top of his voice.

'What happens now?' Beth demanded.

'You're going to take yourself to a

safe spot while I hunt for Peake,' Adam said fiercely.

'I won't leave you. Where do you think Peake is now?'

'I shall try his home first.'

She linked her arm through his, and they set off along the street. Several men ran past them towards the warehouse as they went on, and suddenly Adam turned and shouted loudly.

'Father, hold up a moment.'

Beth gasped with relief when she recognised Jeremy Traherne. The men with Adam's father stopped and crowded around them, and Jeremy caught hold of Beth's shoulder.

'I thought I told you to stay at home,' he remonstrated.

'Not now,' Adam said. 'Save the recriminations until later. I would still be lying in the fire if it were not for Beth's efforts.'

He gave an account of what had happened, and some of the men turned and ran towards the warehouse, eager to save what they could of the evidence.

'Here is a present for you, Father.'

Adam reached into his coat pocket and produced *Sea Rover*'s log.

'I found that in a desk in Peake's office, just one of many. We lost all hands when *Sea Rover* was wrecked. So do what you can at the warehouse. I have something to do right now that's most important.'

Adam put an arm around Beth's shoulder.

'Get what you can from the fire and guard it well,' he said to his father.

'Take a couple of our men with you,' Jeremy said fiercely. 'I'd come myself but I shan't be able to keep up with you.'

'I can handle this alone,' Adam replied.

Jeremy turned and headed along the street towards the warehouse. Adam and Beth continued on their way. They soon reached the gates of Peake's mansion and turned into the driveway. The house was in darkness, silent and still. Beth led the way to the house, and when they reached the front door Adam pushed her aside gently.

'I don't want you mixed up in this, Beth,' he said firmly. 'You might get hurt. Just leave this to me. I want to take Peake alive, if possible, and I don't need you getting in the way.'

'I'll remain outside,' she said quietly. 'I won't get in your way.'

He knocked at the door and the sounds echoed through the silence. Beth shivered. She was so tired she could hardly stand. She heard the sound of bolts being withdrawn on the inside of the door, and when it was opened a fraction the head of Mrs Fetters appeared.

'What do you want at this hour?' she demanded.

'Is Jonah at home?' Adam enquired. 'I need to tell him that his warehouse is on fire and in danger of burning down.'

Mrs Fetters uttered a cry of shock as she fell back a step. Adam strode forward and entered the house with

Beth close on his heels. Mrs Fetters clutched at Adam's arm and tried to stop him but he shrugged her off.

'Mr Peake is not at home,' she cried. 'He has not been here since this afternoon.'

'I need to search the house for him,' Adam retorted.

He picked up a lamp that was standing on a small table in the hall and went to the drawing-room, thrusting open the door. Beth was at his shoulder when he entered the room, where Matilda Peake sat by the fire.

'What is the meaning of this intrusion?' she gasped.

'It is imperative that I see Jonah,' Adam said. 'Have you any idea where he might be?'

'I have no knowledge of his business or movements. Please leave my house at once.'

Adam turned and began a search of the house, Beth remaining at his side throughout. They found no sign of Peake, and Adam faced Beth at the end of the search, shaking his head as he regarded her.

'I shall have to go through the whole town looking for him,' he said determinedly. 'I can't stop now, Beth.'

'I wouldn't want you to,' she replied. 'And I'll go with you every step of the way.'

She broke off as the front door was thrust open and a man entered. Adam turned swiftly, and Beth saw her brother, Nick.

'What are you two doing here?' Nick demanded, slamming the door at his back and leaning against it.

'I think you should answer that question.'

Adam went forward to confront Nick.

'You fired a shot at us and Peake took us prisoner.'

'But that shot didn't hit you.' Nick grinned. 'I could have killed you if I had been loyal to Peake.'

'Where is Peake now?' Beth demanded. 'You've got to make up your mind here and now just where you stand, Nick. Do you know that two men are at Sedge Manor with orders to kill Father if Peake sends the order?'

'I don't believe it.'

'Peake told me that is the situation at Sedge Manor.'

Beth went to Nick's side, grasped him by the shoulders and shook him.

'Peake is finished. We have proof of his smuggling and wrecking. If you know what is good for you then go home, save Father from those men, and stay there until Peake has been captured.'

Nick shook his head doubtfully. Beth sighed impatiently and turned away from him.

'What are you doing here, Nick?' Adam demanded. 'Are you still running errands for Peake?'

'What if I am?'

'Cresse did the same for years and now he's dead. Is that what's going to happen to you? Answer my question. What are you doing here?'

'I've come to collect a bag from the library.'

Nick sighed heavily, his defiance ebbing slowly.

'Where are you to see Peake with the bag?'

'He's at the Lobster Pot with Jaime Spencer. His coach is at the back of the barn there, and he's off to Falmouth to supervise the taking of your ship, *Seagull*.'

Nick's face was purpling under Adam's grip, and Adam suddenly released him. Nick fell helplessly to the floor, gasping for air.

'You'd do well to follow Beth's advice and return to Sedge Manor,' Adam said sternly. 'I'll go along to the Lobster Pot and talk to Peake, and I'll pick up a couple of my father's men on the way.'

He looked into Beth's eyes.

'This time I'll want no argument from you, Beth,' he added. 'It could prove to be too dangerous for your presence.'

'I'll get back to the manor,' Nick

said, straightening. 'I'll do what is right, Beth.'

He opened the door and hurried out into the gloom. Adam followed, with Beth in close attendance, and the door slammed behind them with great violence. Beth was surprised to see that dawn was breaking.

'Where do I leave you in safety, Beth?'

Adam stopped in the shelter of a creaking tree by Peake's big gate and drew her into his arms, placing his mouth close to her ear. The wind tore at them, and Beth shivered. Her exhaustion was such that she could barely think straight.

'Let's keep going together,' she responded.

Adam opened the gate and they went on. They would have to pass Peake's warehouse on their way to the Lobster Pot and Adam intended taking two of his father's men with him. He held Beth close to his left side as they continued, and his keen gaze, accustomed to the vast stretches of the ocean, was adjusted to the close darkness about them. The moon enabled him to see ahead for several yards, and when he heard the sound of running feet coming towards them he pulled Beth into a doorway and they huddled in the shadows.

Moments later, several men went running by, and Adam was startled when he recognised one as Jonah Peake. Before he could react, the men had gone, but then a straggler came panting along and Adam stepped out of cover to confront him.

'What's causing all the excitement?' Adam demanded.

The man paused thankfully and bent over, gasping for breath, his shoulders heaving. Adam shook him impatiently.

'There's word that *Seagull* is heading into the bay from Falmouth and one of Peake's ships is waiting for her. There's going to be a battle.'

The man straightened, peering closely into Adam's face.

'Hey, you're Adam Traherne!' he gasped.

Adam struck the man with a clenched fist, felling him to the ground. He grasped Beth and drew her out of the doorway.

'Come on, Beth, we've got to see this.'

They went back along the street with renewed vigour, galvanised by the news. Passing Peake's mansion, they continued to the end of the street where the cliff started, and the light of the moon gave them a perfect view of the bay. The storm had not abated and the violent sea was still rough. The roar of wind and waves was overwhelming.

Adam could see Peake and a knot of men standing, gazing out to sea. He drew Beth to one side and sheltered her with his body. Beth recognised Peake's voice and peered at him, her face concealed by Adam's arm.

'Someone light a fire,' Peake shouted, and two of his men moved swiftly to obey.

'Look at the ship out there,' Adam said in a low tone, and Beth lifted a hand to her eyes to cut off the wind and blinked as she looked at the black shape of the ship she had seen earlier. 'That's Peake's ship,' Adam continued, 'and by the look of her I'd say she's in trouble. There's no sign of Seagull yet, if she is coming, and that ship is dragging her anchor. She's been blown towards the rocks at Needle Point. If the crew doesn't act in the next few minutes then nothing will be able to save her.'

Beth watched, filled with a terrible fascination. She could see the ship moving towards the shore, and there seemed to be no movement aboard. Peake was shouting loudly, as if he could be heard across that wild expanse of stormy sea. But the ship went on, helpless in the grip of wind and water.

Flames crackled nearby as a man started a fire, and Adam led Beth around the group surrounding Peake, until their vision was no longer impaired by the leaping flames.

'Those fools aboard my ship are asleep,' Peake raged.

'There's nothing they can do,' Adam said to Beth. 'They're on a lee shore. They can't get the wind to help them off, and the waves are against them. It's only a matter of time.'

'What about *Seagull*?' Beth asked. 'Did you know she was coming from Falmouth?'

'No. I expect the crew made temporary repairs and sailed to prevent a further attempt against her. Rufus Mull is a good man and wouldn't risk the ship. I don't expect *Seagull* to enter the bay in this storm. She'll stay clear of the coast and ride out the bad weather.'

Beth was watching the doomed ship heading faster and faster towards inevitable destruction. The roaring of the sea was ceaseless, the howling of the wind sounding like a dirge screeching for the souls of those men trapped aboard the ship.

The end came quickly. Massive waves lifted and rolled the ship in a surging rush towards the black rocks. The ship was suddenly halted as if a giant hand had seized it, and such was the noise of the storm that those on the cliff did not hear the sound of the terrific impact. The ship remained upright for a split second then keeled over, inundated by crashing waves. Blinding spray flew over her, concealing her outline, and the next instant she was gone, her bottom torn out, the sea claiming her.

Beth turned away and pressed her face against Adam's chest, trying to wipe the horror of the scene from her mind. She could hear Peake's hated voice bewailing the loss of his ship, but not once did he mention the drowned crew. Adam put his arms around her slender shoulders, comforting her silently while the wind raged about them.

'I need Peake to leave these men,' Adam said in Beth's ear. 'I can't tackle him while he has so much help at hand.'

Beth peered under Adam's arm and looked at the group around Peake.

Adam turned her away.

'Don't look in that direction,' he advised. 'If we're recognised it will be the end of us. I'm hoping some of my father's men will have heard the news of the ships and come up here to see for themselves. If there is a fight, Beth, then get well clear of it. Do you promise?'

'I promise,' she repeated.

More men were arriving on the cliff and all joined the group around Peake. Beth was dispirited by the sight, fearing that the odds against Adam were too great for his success. Then she saw a man limping towards the group and realised with a shock that it was Jeremy Traherne.

'Adam,' she gasped, 'there's your father!'

Adam glanced over his shoulder, pushing Beth away.

'Keep clear,' he said quickly, and ran towards Jeremy.

At that moment, Peake looked around and recognised the old sea captain.

'There's Jeremy Traherne, men,' he shouted. 'Take him. Throw him over the cliff.'

His words triggered off a confusion of action. Beth, staring wide-eyed in shock, saw two men start towards Jeremy, but others in the group around Peake started fighting with Peake's men, one of them attempting to seize Peake and hold him. Adam reached his father's side and stood between him and the men trying to seize him. He felled one man, but a second ducked under his flailing fists and grappled with Jeremy, who lost his balance and fell to the ground.

Beth ran forward and grasped the man wrestling with Jeremy. She grasped a handful of his hair and tugged with all her strength. The man rolled away, then sprang up, and Jeremy produced a pistol, aimed at the man and fired. There was a sharp cry of pain and the man fell on his face. Jeremy lumbered to his feet and went forward into the group of fighting men, swinging his heavy pistol by its barrel.

Beth looked around. Adam was fighting three men who were endeavouring to pinion his arms, and Beth was scared that all four might pitch over the edge of the cliff. She rushed to Adam's aid, and received a swinging blow on the head that sent her headlong. Dazed, she staggered to her feet to find herself confronted by Peake, who was swinging a pistol. He grasped her left arm with an unbreakable grip. In the background, the sound of several pistol shots rang out and vague figures fell in the night.

'You again!' Peake snarled. 'I wish I'd never set eyes on you.'

A man approached with levelled gun, and Beth recognised Peter Radcliffe, the exciseman. Relief filled her, for if the men of the customs had been alerted then Peake was finished.

'Jonah Peake, I am arresting you on suspicion of smuggling. Release that woman and surrender yourself.'

Peake uttered a curse and pulled

Beth to him, encircling her waist, intent upon using her as a shield.

'Get back or I'll go over the cliff and take her with me,' Peake cried.

Adam came dashing forward. He grasped Beth around the waist and crashed his right fist against Peake's jaw. Peake staggered. Beth felt his hold on her slacken momentarily, then tightened again, and he began to pull her towards the edge of the cliff, now only feet away. Peake was shouting at the top of his voice. Beth tried to break his grip, but his arm was like steel.

Adam struck Peake again and the man staggered. His weight took him backwards even closer to the cliff edge. Beth felt panic sweep through her. She was helpless in his grip, and could see the white water of crashing waves far below. Already she could feel a sense of falling through dark space, and closed her eyes as dizziness swirled through her senses.

Jeremy appeared beside them, swinging the pistol he was gripping. The heavy butt struck Peake's forehead and felled him instantly. Peake's hold on Beth was broken and Adam dragged her away from the cliff edge. Jeremy staggered and almost went over the cliff. He threw himself aside and rolled back to safety, but Peake went over backwards, his feet moving frantically as he tried to regain his balance, until there was no more cliff beneath him and he fell with a scream into the boiling inferno awaiting below.

Beth closed her eyes, her mind protesting at the horrors that had engulfed them since Adam's return. Adam lifted her gently to her feet and she felt better with his strong arms around her.

'Peake has gone,' Adam said softly, kissing her ear. 'And with his passing, this evil is at an end.'

'No,' she said faintly. 'There's still Father. Peake's men are with him. They have orders to kill him.'

'Not them,' Jeremy looked up beside them. 'When you came to me earlier, the first thing I did was send some men to Sedge Manor, and one of them reported to me a few minutes ago that your father is all right. He regained his senses this afternoon. Peake's men ran off.'

He looked around, grinning broadly.

'It looks as if the law is taking control here so what say we go home?'

Adam felt Beth sag a little, and swung her up into his arms. He kissed her ardently.

'Sweet Beth,' he whispered in her ear. 'I do believe the worst is over at last. If you still have a mind to wed me then I suggest we start laying our plans. The future awaits us. This storm is passing, and with it the evil of Jonah Peake. His shadow has gone. Everything will be fine now. What say you, my dearest?'

'Yes,' she murmured happily, her mind clearing, and she was aware that the future would be fine in so many ways.

Sister Dominique, already having serious doubts about her calling, is sent on a mercy mission to South America after a devastating earthquake. There, she meets Dr Steve Daniels, and feelings she had never expected to experience again are stirred up. As she is thrown into caring for a relentless stream of casualties, her thoughts are in turmoil. How will she cope in the outside world if she leaves the sisterhood? And dare she allow herself to fall in love again?

HOUSE OF FEAR

Phyllis Mallett

Jill's twenty-first birthday is more than just a milestone — it marks the day her life changes forever . . . A letter arrives on the morning of her birthday; an invitation to travel to Crag House on the remote Scottish island of Inver to stay with the grandfather whose existence she had been completely unaware of. Whilst there, she meets her cousins, Owen and George, and handsome neighbour Robert Cameron. But her visit has involved her in a web of deceit that may threaten her life . . .

SUSPICIOUS HEART

Susan Udy

When Erin discovers that her mother's home and livelihood is under threat from the disturbingly handsome Sebastian, she knows she has to fight his plans every step of the way. However, she quickly realises Sebastian is equally determined to win, and he apparently has the backing of the entire village. When a campaign of intimidation is begun against Erin and her mother, it doesn't take her long to work out that it can only be Sebastian behind it . . .